WHAT LUCK, THIS LIFE

# WHAT LUCK, THIS LIFE

## KATHRYN SCHWILLE

HUB CITY PRESS

SPARTANBURG, SC

Cover Artwork © The Woodbine Workshop
Book Design: Meg Reid
Proofreaders: Kalee Lineberger and Mary-Peyton Crook
Printed in Dexter, MI by Thomson-Shore

## Library of Congress Cataloging-in-Publication Data

Schwille, Kathryn.
What luck, this life / Kathryn Schwille.
Spartanburg : Hub City Press, 2018.
LCCN 2018006016 (print) | LCCN 2017061677 (ebook)
ISBN 9781938235429 (hardback) | ISBN 9781938235436 (e-book)
LCSH: Family life—Fiction. | Social problems—Fiction.
Small cities—Texas—Fiction. Columbia (Spacecraft)—Accidents—Fiction.
LCC PS3619.C496 (print) | LCC PS3619.C496 W53 2018 (ebook)
DDC 813/.6—dc23
LC record available at https://lccn.loc.gov/2018006016

This project is supported in part by an award
from the National Endowment for the Arts.

186 W. Main Street
Spartanburg, SC 29306
864-327-8515
www.hubcity.org

*for Tom, who believed.*

"...we enquired of the destiny of the universe, and the oracles of thermodynamics answered us; every existing form will break up in a blaze of heat; there is no entity can escape the irretrievable disorder of the corpuscles; time is a catastrophe, perpetual and irreversible."

*from* **ITALO CALVINO, "IMPLOSION"**

# CONTENTS

# FM 104

Coyotes, weasels, green flies, crows. The animals heard it first. Along the weedy edge of Route 20, a turkey buzzard quit the possum she'd lucked into and took cover in a stand of pines. The wild pig under Cecil Dawson's oak trees snorted twice and froze. To us, it came from out of nowhere: two blasts and the roar of a crashing train that rumbled far too long. Our windows rattled, our floorboards quivered, our breakfasts trembled on their tables. We thought terror, we thought bombs, we thought of our loved ones. A few of us thought to scream. Those of us who ran outside, the ground beneath us shaking still, saw wobbling plumes of smoke in a Texas postcard sky. Some saw three trails, some claim one. No one saw the fire balls, since they streaked west of here. Jimmy Hubble counted the seconds, like the time between lightning and thunder. One thousand one, one thousand ten, one thousand thirty. Over the trees of his south pasture, pieces of something fell from the sky. Grover Sharkey heard a whizzing sound, like a bullet flying past. Carter Bostic heard a thud on her roof, then another, then two more. We turned on our televisions. Columbia's lost, the anchor said. Not lost, we said, it's here. Cable on a hay bale, computer in a tree, space suit in a briar patch, toilet by a school. Beside Junior Pierce's mail box lay a shoeless foot, missing one big toe. Didn't anything burn up? On the shoulder of Farm-to-Market 104, Lila MacFarland reached for a square of silver metal, big as a turkey platter, charred on just one side. The heat it gave off reddened her palm. She made a hot pad out of two old towels and laid it in her trunk. Don't touch anything, the anchor said. Chemicals, danger, NASA doesn't know. Arthur Kenny smelled something in the air, but he could not describe it. Not fuel, not smoke, nor burning flesh. Not the East Texas perfumes he knew: creosote, fertilizer, pulpwood, pines. His dog held something in her mouth; Arthur's legs went weak. Here, Dingo, bring it here. She circled, teased and dropped it on his shoe. A black piece of pipe, narrow as a woman's finger. Good girl, he said, and chained her to a tree. What could we do? The stuff was everywhere, light as paper, heavy as brick. We set up roadblocks where it littered our highways. Our children played at searching. For what? A nose cone? A fuel cell? An instrument panel? Coyotes, weasels, green flies, crows. For weeks we walked with our heads down. Watching, watching, where we walked.

# BOSTIC'S

**B**ostic's was a corner store on a two-lane highway, a location that should have made for good commerce. The traffic on 91 was never heavy—deep East Texas was too lightly populated for that—but the highway ran out to Minden Lake, where the bass were lunkers and the campgrounds rarely empty. From Bostic's gravel parking lot where the fussy gas pumps stood, it was just a mile to the road that led to Kiser.

In the rising light of a cool October morning, Carter Bostic struggled at the store's back door, fuming over the lock she'd begged Roy weeks ago to fix. Maybe today was the day she'd call up to Eno for the locksmith to come, and with that money wasted when Roy could so easily do it himself, his attention might settle on the things that cried out for doing. He had held her up after breakfast, talking about what money they didn't have and apparently never would, until finally she had to leave him there in the dirt path that passed for a driveway at their place. She'd sped off in the Silverado he'd picked up from the dealer the morning of 9/11—two years old and the light of Roy's life. While the Twin Towers were collapsing, Roy had tooled around Kiser showing off their big purchase. Now they could barely make the payments.

Carter pushed in on the key, pulled back, turned slowly. Nothing. Roy had insisted on the deadbolt, though she'd told him it would never keep out trouble determined to get in. Last year, someone had broken in through a window and stolen cigarettes, shotgun shells and four bottles of iodine from the back room where Carter kept the horse supplies. The cigarettes and shells didn't bother her, but nobody needed that much iodine unless they were cooking meth.

She tried the key with both hands. Yesterday that had worked, but not today. Inside her purse, her cell phone rang. Behind her, she heard footsteps.

"Graphite?" Grady MacFarland held out a pencil.

"If Roy doesn't fix this lock."

"You'll what? Here, let me. Answer your phone." Grady took the key and ran the pencil over its teeth. He was not much taller than Carter, the wiry sort that Roy would call scrawny. This morning she could see gray around the temples in his light brown hair, but he was one of those men who would be slow to age. The crow's feet around his green eyes would not deter a younger woman, if he fancied one.

She let the phone ring. "So what are you needing this time of the morning?"

"No more than your sweet hello. And some batteries." Grady put the key in the lock and when the door opened Carter gave him the smile he'd flattered her for. She'd known Grady MacFarland since she was fourteen and for a while in high school he'd shared with her his hopes and dreams and plenty more on the old plaid sofa in his parents' downstairs den. Whatever else they'd been— right for each other but at the wrong time, or wrong for each other and lucky enough to find out—they were still friends. He had the soul of an intellect and why he'd given up on life in Tulsa to come back here, she had yet to figure out. He'd bought a piece of land near his mother, an insurance business, and just last week, two of Jimmy Hubble's brood mares. Carter was, herself, fed up with Kiser and fed up with family obligation. It had hogtied Roy and tethered them to this store forever.

"Coffee'll be ready soon," she said.

Grady held the door for her. "Coffee? That's new." A shaving nick on his jaw was fresh. The aftershave was lime.

"Roy's idea. Maybe it'll help. You know Roy. He can always think of something else for me to do."

So far, at fifty cents a cup, they were just breaking even. The one financial bright spot Carter could see was a call yesterday from Jerome, her old boss at Porta-Chow. Last February, after the space shuttle broke up and hundreds of people arrived to search for debris, Porta-Chow came in from Kansas City and set up barbecue pits and trailers with portable kitchens. They hired thirty locals. Every afternoon Carter left the store at three o'clock and went to work at four, prepping vegetables and serving up the meats. In twenty-two days she'd made three thousand dollars. Now Porta-Chow was setting up in Baton Rouge, where a tornado had just come through. "We could use you," Jerome had said.

Carter slid her purse under the counter and unlocked the front door. She'd told Jerome she would think about it. She hadn't mentioned it to Roy; she knew what he would say.

Outside, Junior Pierce had pulled up his cab to the diesel tank. The sun was breaking through the clouds right into his eyes, and he shaded them as he looked out over the scrubby pasture at the intersection with Buford Road. Not even cattle grazed in the weeds where Pizza Hut had wanted to build, and didn't, because Horace Chadwick, rich enough and happy with the status quo, wouldn't sell. Last week, the pizza chain had announced it would build in Eno and the old description of Kiser had bubbled up again: twenty miles south of Eno and thirty years behind.

Carter said a quick prayer that the diesel pump would hold out long enough to fill Junior's tank. She started the coffee and opened the last new pack of Styrofoam cups. Maybe there was no point in buying more.

"Grady," she called, "you ever seen a white birch tree? I've been telling Roy we should travel. We could get someone to look after the horses and the store. He says there's nowhere he wants to go. How can that be? Nowhere."

"Man knows what he wants. You got any fire lighters?"

"Got these butane lighters up here. It's just that I've never seen a birch tree, I've never seen more than three inches of snow. I want to see the prairie that Willa Cather wrote about in this book I'm reading. You ever read her? I'm not afraid to go alone. I swear I'm not. I'd get on the train with a good book and talk to strangers who sat next to me. A stranger might be nice once in a while, instead of these old boys come in here that I been knowing all my life."

Grady had wandered into the back room and was walking out with two tubes of horse wormer. He stopped in front of the drug store supplies.

"Not you," Carter said. "I'm not talking about you." Grady seemed to be looking at the condoms, though more likely it was razor blades. He had married his college sweetheart and the rumor was they'd had a happy life, though one without children. Three years ago they'd split up. As far as Carter knew, he hadn't had a single date since he moved back to Kiser. Maybe he was carrying a torch. "You know where the batteries are?" she said. "Over by the window, next to the light bulbs." She fished into her purse for a Tums. Roy had taught her never to rush the customers, but she wanted Grady out of here, before Newland Sparks came in. Newland was running his foul mouth when no one else was in the store, about how much she wanted to give him pussy, what would happen when she did. It left her feeling the need for a shower and not ever in the mood for sex, as Roy had taken to pointing out. If Newland came in, Grady would stay until he left, thinking he could keep the creep in line. But Newland would just come back later and that meant two encounters in a day instead of one. It was making her stomach hurt, a slow burn right in the pit. She'd just as soon Newland Sparks come in now, get his jerk-ass crap over with, go shoot off his rocks if that was what he did after and she could maybe—maybe—have a little peace for the rest of the day. She'd tried to get Roy to do something. "You keep your mouth shut," he'd told her. "All that kin Newnie's got around here. We can't keep open if even half of them turn against us." Carter had lived all her life in Chireno County. If she woke up tomorrow in another state and never saw this store again, it would be an answer to prayers. Once she and Roy had driven to Tennessee. It seemed like a nice place.

Grady set the batteries and horse wormer on the counter. He saw her watching out the window. "Newland still bothering you?"

"It should be against the law, what he's doing. Sheriff's deputy that was in here last week, Cecil Dawson, I told him I got a gun and I'm not afraid to use it. I'd just as soon shoot Newland Sparks as shoot a bug." She handed Grady his change, setting the coins firmly in his slender palm. "Put me in jail, put me away. At least I'd have three meals a day and a roof over my head. And he'd be dead."

Junior Pierce had come up to the register, and now he was holding out a hundred dollar bill. "Let's hope not," he said.

"You know I'm just running my mouth," Carter said. "That all you got?"

"Sorry, this is it. Sparks, the poor bastard. Black sheep of the clan."

"They've bailed him out often enough, is what I've heard," Carter said. Maybe Newland was like a zit to the family, a blight they wished would go away, but they had not abandoned him. There were the comfortable Sparks and the struggling Sparks, but they were all Sparks.

"Where you headed, Junior?" Carter asked.

"Eno. Picking up a load of Brangus. After I stop at Walmart."

Carter frowned.

"You just ruined her day," Grady said.

"I'm looking to buy a cell phone." Junior craned his neck in a mock survey of the store. "Don't see none of those in here."

"Long as that's all you buy." Carter opened a new bundle of tens and counted out Junior's change. "Roy says that Pizza Hut would have doubled up our business."

"Good old Horace," Grady said. "Like they say, nothing wrong with Kiser that a few funerals wouldn't fix."

"Trouble is," Junior said, "his sons aren't no different." He stuffed the tens into his wallet, which he slipped into the pocket of a leather jacket so new Carter could smell it in the air that stirred when he turned to go. Some people were doing okay.

Grady dropped two quarters in the coffee tin. "Grandbaby coming soon?"

"Two more weeks at least," Carter said. "You know how first babies are." Or maybe he didn't, with none of his own. At forty, Carter was startled by the granny talk. She still had a pretty good figure—a little thicker in the middle now, but she looked okay in a pair of jeans with a top tucked in. Roy encouraged her to show off her ass. "But mostly I'm sitting down," she would tell him. "You stand up often enough," he said. "You got to pull the lever up front to clear the pumps." Carter drew the line at cleavage, but she wore the clingy tops that Roy liked to buy her. Her breasts were still finely shaped, though she thought them a bit small.

Grady took two noisy sips from his coffee. He'd always been a slurper. "You want me to stay for a while, in case Newland shows up?"

"I know you got things to do. The creep doesn't scare me. Anyhow, I see Teeter Minkins out there. He'll be in soon as he tells Junior about the whopper bass he caught last week." Grady was looking at her, like he was trying to figure, stay or go. She was wearing a V-neck top; maybe he was admiring. "Really," she said. "I'll be fine."

"You need me, you call me. I'll be at the barn."

She watched him go. If it were Grady MacFarland she were married to instead of Roy Bostic, she wouldn't be in this fix. Carter opened her Cather book and read about winter settling in over the Divide.

❋ ❋ ❋

Early in the morning, most of the customers at Bostic's store were men—truck drivers stopping in before they hit the road, or farmers and small-time ranchers hoping to skip the drive to town. As towns went, Kiser didn't offer much. It was the county seat to a friendly place that fortune had not smiled on. A few antebellum houses stood on the outskirts of town because cotton had once been king, but that heyday expired with the arrival of spindle pickers that worked best on flat land. The softly rolling hills of East Texas had lost out, and the tide of America's industrial prosperity did not come again. The logging trucks that rumbled past Bostic's were headed to mills in other places. The six smelly poultry farms north of town sent every chicken to Eno for slaughter. Kiser was left with a shrinking population, a stagnant tax base and people on the public dole. The new mayor called welfare the town's biggest employer.

Carter had tried working at the Tyson plant when she and Roy were first married. She'd been a plucker. The money was paltry and after six months, when her wrists and shoulders began to give out, Roy persuaded her to quit. Then the three babies came, and now there was the store. Porta-Chow had been a dream compared to the store. There were rules at Porta-Chow: no alcohol, no swearing, no dates with the crews who were searching for shuttle debris. Jerome was fair, and people who broke the rules were dealt with. After Jodie Tulane took a married firefighter from Oklahoma home with her, Jerome fired her and got his whole outfit sent home. Jerome was a good boss by Carter's standards, one who laughed easily and treated people like they mattered. He'd let Carter bring in a radio to get the good country station from Shreveport, though Jerome—a black man with roots in East St. Louis—didn't care for the music. One day Carter wore a white ball cap that she'd given to Roy but he'd never worn, and she got the idea to have an astronaut sign it. Jerome said that was okay, so when Air Force Colonel Charles Bradley came through the food line, she asked him. He'd flown one of the Columbia shuttle flights and he had a kind face, though she could see he was grieving. When he handed the cap back to her the next day, there were eight astronaut signatures on it. She figured the cap was worth some money now, and she thought of it like an ace in the hole. She wanted to help Beth and Dave with the baby, maybe buy a nice stroller. If Roy didn't let her go to Louisiana, she was going to get on eBay and sell the cap. It would break her heart.

"Something's on your mind." Teeter Minkins plopped a bottle of headache pills on the counter and looked Carter over with approval. She gave him a smile, though no amount of feminine charms would result in him having more money to spend. His diabetic wife waddled on given-out knees and Teeter wasn't in great shape himself.

"You smelled the wood burning?" she said. "I'm just wondering what to fix Roy for his supper." Over Teeter's shoulder, through the front window, she saw Newland Sparks looking in, laughing at something. He had a loud laugh and a speech impediment. His r's didn't come out hard enough, like baby-talk. *Caw-teh*, and even his own last name: *Spawks*. No one mocked him, and that was a sure sign no one liked him. Last week he'd discovered a new way to torture Carter. She'd taken out an ad in the Penny Pincher, hoping to to sell her Halloween decorations and the costumes she didn't need any more since the kids were grown. The phone number she gave was for her new cell and now Newland Sparks had it. He'd called at least four times, from different phones so she'd think it was someone about the ad. He always hung up without speaking, but she knew it was him.

"Teeter," Carter said. "Get you a cup of coffee and stay a while." Maybe it was better to have company. Newland might give up and go do something else.

"Eleanor's bad off," Teeter said. "I ought to get these pills home to her."

"A cup on the house? I just brewed it."

"I guess one cup wouldn't hurt. Her blood pressure's high, and it gives her these headaches. Between that and the diabetes, keeps her running to the doctor."

Newland slinked through the door. The pit in Carter's stomach burned more. "Who's she go to?"

"Doc Meadows."

"Roy used to go to him. He didn't like him." Meadows was married to a Sparks, a pretty woman named Beryl. Half the town went to him because he didn't charge as much and didn't run as many tests. Roy thought he was lazy.

"I owe him too much to change off now," Teeter said. "Besides, Eleanor likes him." He lowered his voice. "Though he got some slime for kin."

Newland came towards the register with a pack of Bugles. He laid two dollar bills on the counter and fixed Carter in his sights. "Carter looks mighty nice today, don't she, Teeter?"

"Carter looks nice every day."

"I had a dream about Carter last night. Want to hear about my dream, Carter?"

"I don't want to hear it." She dropped the change into his hand and leaned over to turn on the little radio at the end of the counter.

Newland fastened his gaze on her chest. "Nice, juicy dream."

Teeter stopped stirring the sweetener into his coffee. He looked at the floor, where his work boots splayed out in the duck stance his bad hip engendered. "I believe you ought to keep that stuff to yourself," he said. "She said she doesn't want to hear it."

"She was wearing some of them thong panties. Black ones. I bet she's got 'em on now."

Teeter pulled the little stirrer out of his cup and pointed it at Newland. "That's not nice," he said. "To be saying that kind of thing to her."

Newland looked at the headache pills Teeter had set on the counter. "Real juicy dream," he said. The first word came out *weel*. "Real results. Know what I mean?" Teeter put the pills in his pocket. Beneath the stubble on his cheeks the skin grew red.

Carter called out to Jimmy Hubble, who'd come through the door and was headed for the auto supplies. "Hey, there's fresh coffee over here."

Jimmy's head disappeared as he squatted down. "I'm looking for the wiper fluid."

"We're all out," Carter said. The shelves were so dusty down there. "We got an order coming in next week." No one had bought any wiper fluid in a year. They'd stopped ordering it.

"Hell, Carter, that won't help me today."

"Aw, just put some water in there," Newland said. "That'll do just as good."

Teeter snapped a plastic cover on his cup. "You're so full of it," he said. He turned to Carter with a sheepish look. "I got to get home."

"I know. Tell Eleanor I hope she's better soon. You come on back when you can stay."

Newland started talking about the dream again.

"Knock it off," Jimmy said. He put two packs of gum down hard on the counter. "Carter doesn't want to hear that shit."

Newland took his eyes off Carter and glared at Jimmy. "How's your brother? How's Carl?" Jimmy's brother had once been married to Newland's half-sister. Rumor was he had an itchy fist.

Jimmy turned his back on Newland and handed Carter a ten. "Carl couldn't be happier. I'll tell him you asked."

"Don't rush off, Jimmy," Carter said. "How about a cup of coffee?"

"Some other time." Jimmy ripped the tab on a pack of gum and shoved a stick into his mouth. "Too crowded in here."

Before Jimmy was out the door, Newland started in again.

"Stop it," Carter said. But he ran on, talking about titties and his dick against her thigh. *Cawteh you make me hawd.* Her legs grew weak and the knot in her stomach twisted like a snake. She pretended to dust under the counter and kept her head down until Mitzi Gander came in with her two little boys and Newland left. Carter pulled the pack of Tums from her purse and popped two. Mitzi set a carton of milk and a box of tampons on the counter. "Too much Mexican dinner?"

"Too much Newland Sparks," Carter said.

"Oh, that. Can't Roy do something?"

"If he doesn't, I will."

Roy Bostic had lived all his life in Chireno County, so a drive to the next county for beer did not seem odd. The Baptists had a choke hold on East Texas. The rest of Texas laughed, and called it the hundred miles of dry. Roy would split the Friday beer run with friends and this week, thank God, it was someone else's turn. He was beat. His doctor had told him he had gout, and that was why his big toe felt like there was gravel sticking in it. He limped into the house. With work over, he didn't have to suck it up and pretend.

Carter wasn't home, and he hoped that meant she was buying groceries. They were out of everything. She'd called him at the warehouse to apologize for driving off in a huff this morning, but he suspected the real reason she'd called was to let him know that Newland Sparks had been in again. Roy didn't like what Sparks was doing, but the guy was basically harmless. Someday he'd find someone else to bug.

Roy popped a beer and scrounged around for the package of crackers going stale in the back of the pantry. In the den, he turned on the clumsy computer and watched it dial up the online medical world. He'd never known anyone with gout. He thought it was a disease of fat old men.

Carter came in a half-hour later, no grocery bags in sight. She set her purse on the table next to him. "If your toe's hurting, you shouldn't be having that beer."

"Where've you been?" He flipped off the website he was on.

"Reba was late for her shift again. I tried to call, but the line was tied up. I figured you were on the computer." For once she didn't say he ought to turn on his cell phone because otherwise why have it.

"We needed groceries," he said.

"You could have stopped for groceries. When you went over to Phil's to get the beer you had to pass Brookshire's twice."

"But you always buy the groceries."

"Because you never do."

Carter turned on her heel and headed for the kitchen. He heard her rummaging in the cupboard and figured she'd find the bow-tie pasta in there. He wasn't in the mood for pasta. She would open a can of tomatoes and dump a lot of cheese on it and the whole thing would go straight to their waistlines.

Inside Carter's purse, her cell was ringing. "Let it ring," she called. "I'll be right there." He pulled out the phone and answered. It was Jerome.

"She's not interested," he said. "I appreciate your calling but she's going to be tied up. Our daughter's having a baby."

Carter came in. "Is that Jerome? Let me talk to him."

"I'm sorry," Roy said into the phone, turning away from her as she reached for it. "I don't know. Yeah, it's just bad timing for her. Appreciate your calling." He hung up.

"You told him no? I told you to let me talk to him."

"Why didn't you tell me he'd asked? You should have just told him no straight out. We're doing inventory tomorrow so we can get it done before the baby comes."

"Since when? Give me the phone. You were rude. Why shouldn't I go to Baton Rouge? We need the money."

"We don't need it that bad. There are people down there you don't need to be around." He talked on about crime and city blight and for emphasis he used the n-word.

"Don't say that word. You just hung up on one of the most respectable men I know."

"So maybe he's not like a lot of them. But we can't afford to hire somebody to cover for you in the store."

"Which just proves we're not making any money and never will. Inventory? You just made that up."

"We're doing it tomorrow. Sunday, too. We talked about it last week."

"You said you were thinking about it. I thought you had to work."

"I'll be done by noon. I told you that."

"No, you didn't."

Carter stalked into the kitchen. He heard her running water into the pot for pasta, probably twice as much as she needed. It would take forever to boil. He stayed on the computer, looking for a new doctor. There was one over in Toledo Bend he hadn't heard of so he wrote down the phone number. He was only forty-one; he felt like his body was moving toward ruin.

A cross the highway from Bostic's store, high on a grassy knoll in Horace Chadwick's weedy pasture, a clump of rocks poked out where the members of Spring Creek Baptist Church liked to gather for Easter sunrise service. Pastor Will Simpson would take his place on the granite and face west toward Truman Wally's dilapidated barn, grateful he could skip a hot sanctuary blotted by twice-a-year comers. A mile behind him, as the choir sang the sun into the sky, light would break through the trees into the brown waters of the Atoka River, nothing left of its Ayish past but Indian legend and white man's guilt. To the pastor's left, seventeen miles away, was Yellowpine Reservoir, a man-made flooding that sixty years before had covered twenty-odd buildings, scores of junk cars and the unmarked graves of six black families. A sprinkle of boaters would be there at sunrise on Easter, trading Jesus for sport. Pastor Simpson, acknowledging so much of the Lord's work still to be done, would raise his arms to the sky and declare that the Maker had blessed them all with a front row seat to the miracle of resurrection.

On a different Sunday morning, also at sunrise but weeks before Easter, Air Force Col. Charles Bradley had climbed the grassy knoll and looked out over the torn bits of a splendid, gargantuan, trouble-prone spacecraft. It had been his privilege to fly this particular dream of man, a collection of high hopes and low bids. Now a scatter of tiles from its skin lay in the weeds. He thought he could make out something gray that might be the arm of a flight deck chair. He could not remember, at this startling moment, whether the flight deck chairs were gray, or if those were blue. The white box he saw, that he knew. It was part of a cabinet for keeping clothes. Perhaps it had once held his, the golf shirts and shorts he favored in zero gravity. Half a mile from where he stood, though he did not yet know it, was the secluded sanctuary of Spring Creek Baptist, so out of the way that one of its downspouts held a dime bag in transit. In the woods beside the church lay another small bundle, this one much more troubling. It was a handful of flesh that would soon be identified as most of the heart of Mission Specialist Brian Goodwin.

The astronaut walked back to his car, which he'd parked by the gas pumps in front of a low-slung store. He would spend a week in Kiser, driving north to Eno late each night, where a bad mattress in a third-rate motel was his weary haven. He would autograph a ball cap for a friendly woman in the Porta-Chow line, and take it around to the other astronauts, his fellow survivors. It was the least he could do. The people of Kiser had spread their arms around his disaster and accepted the great burden of its grief.

As soon as Carter opened the store the next morning, she called Jerome. "I'll be there Monday," she told him. "I can stay the week." Reba had agreed to sub for her and pull double shifts. That would take more than half of Carter's earnings, but she didn't care. Roy would blow his stack.

Jerome asked if she could stay longer. "I wish," she said. She told him about the baby, and he didn't give her any of the granny business about getting old. Jerome was a professional. But he hadn't minded that she had thanked the searchers, every one of them, every night. "You have a good heart," he told her once, smiling in a way she hadn't seen before. "I try," she said. She'd wished then she could kiss his cheek, because of how hard everyone had worked, because of all they'd been through. Later, when they were cleaning up for the last time, she took off her astronaut cap and put it on Jerome's head. "You're really something," she said.

After Carter hung up, the store was quiet until Roy's friend, Phil, showed up with two men she didn't know. The one they called Mick went in the back where the horse supplies were, brought out a bottle of iodine and handed it to Phil. Phil Lockwood didn't have any animals. He'd bought another bottle only last month. She'd said that night to Roy, "We should take out the iodine. Just not sell it. People can go to town if they need it."

"It's not up to us to police what people do," Roy told her.

"We don't need to make it easier. Phil's your friend. What's he up to? I know he's hard up, but come on."

"If Phil needs money that bad, how else is he going to get it?"

For a while, Carter had kept a list of who bought iodine, figuring maybe the sheriff would want to know. One day a friend of her father's came in. Arthur Kenny, a man she'd looked up to all her life, bought a six-ounce bottle that day and came back for another in two weeks. She gave up the list then.

Now she was ringing up Phil's iodine and two bags of chips, and he wouldn't even look at her. "Jenny doing all right?" she said. His wife was sweet, the quiet type, who had her hands full with three boys.

"She's good," Phil said. "I'll tell her you said hello." The other two were halfway out the door.

After they left, Carter made a list for Baton Rouge: hair net, the new stretch jersey top with the sweetheart neckline, her good jeans. She added the astronaut cap, for old time's sake. Mostly it had sat on her dresser where she could see it every morning, but today she had put it on and stuffed her hair in a pony tail through the back opening. If she was going to sell it soon, she might as well be wearing it. She'd looked again at Col. Bradley's signature—more like printing than cursive. At the one-week remembrance of the disaster at the VFW, Carter had watched his eyes brim with tears he wouldn't let fall. Jenny Lockwood's youngest boy had walked right up to him and handed him a rabbit's foot. "In case you go back up there," Richie said. The colonel thanked him, stroked it once or twice and gave it back. "I might not go again," he said. "Maybe you'll get there."

When Grady came in around ten, Carter couldn't help complaining about Roy. "I'm going to Baton Rouge," she said. "He can't stop me."

"That's no way to be. He thinks it's for your own good."

Carter had gone to the front window to pull the lever on the gas pump. "I'm leaving Monday. I swear." Newland Sparks was outside, just sitting in his truck, looking in. She felt the whole bulky mess of his family. "I hate it here. This store, this job, this town."

"Roy loves you. It counts for something."

"I know." She thought of the rumor that Grady's wife had booted him out. Not everyone lived with someone who loved them. "It's just that Roy is so backward about some things."

"Might be he's afraid." Grady had come over to the window, and now he could see what she was watching. Newland Sparks had gotten out of his truck and was leaning against it, talking on his phone. Six months ago, he wouldn't have had cell coverage this far from town. Then

Sprint came, and Pizza Hut didn't. This place never got what it needed most.

Grady put his arm around Carter's shoulder. She could smell the Tide on his fresh shirt. He was chief of the volunteer fire squad, and when the shuttle came down, he'd become a local hero. He was a good guy, and some other woman was going to make him happy. In high school, though he ran with the college-bound crowd, he'd never let on there was any difference between the two of them. Maybe back then, there wasn't. Maybe she'd had more possibilities than she thought.

Carter's cell phone rang under the counter and when she answered, she heard Newland on the line. "Your hero Grady, he's seeing Sara Farnsworth. How about that, Carter? Another man's wife." She pressed the end button. Grady had followed her to the counter. "Okay," she said into the dead phone. "Okay." Outside, Newland had put his face right up to the window, framing it with his free hand, peering in. He was smiling. Carter shoved the phone into her purse.

"That was quick," Grady said.

Carter picked up a rag and began wiping the counter. "It was Roy. He's on his way in."

"I'll stay 'til he gets here."

"No." She'd said that too fast. Grady looked startled, then hurt. She rubbed harder into the counter. "Roy'll get so pissed when he sees all these coffee stains."

"No? One minute you want my help, the next minute you don't."

"You got stuff to do. I know you do. Plus it's Saturday. Don't you have something planned?" Please, she thought. Tell me you're watching a movie with Gloria Boland or even Jodie Tulane. Some woman who's safely divorced.

"No plans. But it seems like you don't want me here." He glanced out the window.

"It's not that. I'll be fine. Promise."

"Is it Roy? Is he suspicious of me? Because I can talk to him."

"He's in kind of a strange place these days." It wasn't exactly a lie.

Grady looked closely at her. Then he shrugged. "Okay," he said, "but remember what I said."

She watched him walk out and get in his truck, saying something to Newland over his shoulder. Whatever it was, it wouldn't do any good. It might even make things worse. As soon as Grady drove off, Newland came through the door.

"You want to see Roy?" Carter said. "Roy's in the back."

"That's funny. Didn't see Roy's truck."

"He's in the back. He drove in with me."

Newland roamed around the aisles making junior high jokes about Sara Farnsworth. He brought a pack of crackers up to the register. "Don't hear Roy back there," he said. "What's the matter, Carter? Don't want to be alone with me?"

Carter rang up the sale and held out his change. When he grabbed her hand and pulled it to his crotch, pennies spilled to the counter. She was leaning awkwardly across the counter, her head close to his. With his other hand he pulled off her cap, then he let her go.

He was a child with a treasure, grinning like a school-yard bully. Carter reached under the counter for her Glock and held it there. "Give it back," she said.

Newland held her cap in the air, laughing. "Come and get it," he said. When Carter pulled up the gun she aimed for the space between his arm and the floor, but just at that instant, he lowered his hand. The bullet went through the cap where Col. Bradley had signed it, grazing the tip of Newland Sparks's thumb.

Roy hunched on a low stool by the fishing supplies, a laptop warming his knees. He counted the flipping jigs and spinnerbaits, and straightened a row of Trilene. Carter had turned on the coffee maker. Its muffled puts and his laptop's hum gave the air its only life. When his cell rang, Roy hauled himself up and limped outside to where the reception was better. The gout was killing him.

Carter sat cross-legged on the floor, beside the batter-ies. She was writing over the faded price tags with a black pen, careful not to make it look as though the price had been raised. The screen door slammed as Roy came back in, the "Closed" sign rattling behind him. "He's not press-ing charges," he said. "I suppose he'll lord that over us, too. Him and his kin."

Carter reached for another row of batteries and spread them on the floor. "These flashlight batteries are almost expired." She made a pile of the oldest ones. "It's the double A's people buy now, not so much the C's and D's. A lot of things take double A's. I bet we sell three times as many A's as all the others." She set aside two packs of C's.

Roy stood for a time beside Carter and looked about the store. His grandfather had made most of the shelves from two big oaks that fell in a neighbor's back field. Roy had climbed on the shelves when he was small; their fresh-cut smell and sanded edges were a vivid memory. Since he'd taken over the store, he would shop now and then for modern shelving with hooks and nooks and movable parts, only to realize the old shelves were just fine. Probably they could use a good shellacking. It wasn't going to happen now.

Carter's hair had fallen about her face as she leaned over her stacks. He could see her scribbles on the clipboard, the numbers he would have to work at deciphering, the nines that resembled fours. She picked up the batteries she'd set aside. "I'm going to put these in the truck," she said.

"Okay," he said.

She stood for a moment, studying him. The crease he'd noticed lately between her brows was more pronounced today. Shadows rimmed her eyes. "We could still get by," she said.

"I don't know," he said, shifting onto his right foot, the one that wasn't hurting. "I just don't know."

Carter went out, her shirttail a mess of dust from the floor. She moved toward the Silverado, where the harsh October sun, low in the sky, glinted off the hood that hadn't been washed in a month. The day she'd sat with him in the dealer's showroom, jittery about the numbers, flustered over add-ons, they'd agreed right away to order the metallic blue. They thought they would never tire of that, the color of sky. The morning Roy picked up the truck, he'd climbed into the driver's seat, stuck a CD in the changer and turned the music up high. He flew down the highway on top of the world.

# THE ROAD TO HOUSTON

I was born and raised in Kiser, a dinky, third-fiddle town near the Sabine River, a rank and slither-filled water that keeps Texas apart from Louisiana. Kiser had a town square with a courthouse on it, a drugstore, a hardware store, two banks that fought over the town's six wealthy families, a furniture store owned by one of those families and two empty storefronts that the ladies used for bake sales and quilt shows. In the winter of 2003, when Kiser was still my home, my ex-wife Holly had just opened a yoga studio on Main Street. People in town were either proud or leery of her place, depending on their choice of church, and their reaction was one thing Holly and I could still laugh about. We'd been separated six months and we buried the rancor as often as we could for the sake of our son, whose path in life was hard enough. Frankie was eleven, a gifted child who heard voices from the trees and could multiply seven times eight by the time he was six. Where he got all that is anybody's guess. He didn't get it from me.

One Sunday that winter—Groundhog Day to be exact, with no shadow in sight for the critter—I was hiding out in my dreary apartment, avoiding the ruckus that had arrived in Kiser the day before when the shuttle came apart. The town had flown into action—gawking, searching, trying to help—but my altruistic get-up-and-go was tempered by a rawness in my throat and the hangover of a NyQuil slumber. And there was this: I had a big lot of things on my mind. Change had sidled up to me, and more was coming.

With a belly full of orange juice and dubious hope for a clearing head, I reached for the bench chisel next to my chair. A handsome piece of oak lay waiting for me on the floor. In the months since my separation I'd shaped enough heron, deer and hunting dogs to cover the filing cabinet that doubled as a nightstand in the reduced decor of my new life. I'd collected a laundry basket of worthy specimens—my job was foreman for a tree service—but my ideas, not to mention my abilities, fell short of the grace of this striated oak. Fungus and decay had drawn a pink arc through the middle and outlined the arc in purple. There's only one right time to work with a spalted piece like that. Too soon and it's not yet interesting, too late and it's weak and rotten. Someday the piece would speak. A vibration from its next life would reach the conscious me and tell my fingers how to begin.

A phone call from Holly snapped me out of my stupor. She was living with Frankie at her parents' place, a thirty-acre ranchette north of town. Holly didn't call often. I could tell she was bothered; the pitch of her voice was high. "You won't believe this," she said. "What Frankie found." He'd gone out early looking for shuttle fragments. Guiding his pony through heavy brush, he looked up and saw an orange space suit wedged in the crook of a tall tree. There was an astronaut's torso inside it.

"Did you go and see?" I pressed. "Do you know for sure?"

"It's in those trees next to Parkers' place. God, Wes. It's awful."

"A body still intact?"

"Fell out of the sky. Just like that."

"Jesus. Where's Frankie now?" A picture came to mind I didn't much like: Frankie under a tree, looking up.

"Mom's fixing him lunch. If he can eat it. I couldn't. He wanted to go back. I caught him with Dad's binoculars."

"Jesus," I said again. "Hide them."

"Grady says for you to drive over with the bucket truck."

My brother was chief of the volunteer fire department; I understood what he was asking. Someone had to go up in that tree and bring down what was stuck. "Twenty minutes," I said. The company rig was just down the road.

"Wes?"

I knew this tone, a slight drawing out of my short name. Holly was going to change the subject. It was a pattern in our lives, her wanting to talk, and me wanting to duck.

"Grady's your brother and he loves you," she said. "You need to tell him what's going on."

"Right now," I said, "I need to go."

I put an apple in my pocket and grabbed an old pair of gloves I could throw out tomorrow. The dead made me squeamish, something Grady well knew. I'm not like him, steady and rock-solid. He's the most honest man I've ever known. We were in the same state, marriage-wise, but when Eileen fell out of love with him, she just told him. There was no hemming and hawing, no philandering, no telling him she couldn't love him the way she should, this last being what I told Holly. Grady left Eileen, walked away from corporate life in Tulsa, moved back to Kiser and bought a business for himself. He didn't want his old life anymore and he knew it. In Kiser they loved him for that, rejecting the big city. He joined the fire squad and they made him chief right away, though the honeymoon wouldn't last. He's too conscientious for a town like Kiser.

I hadn't spoken to my brother in two weeks, since we'd gotten into it while cooking ribs on Mom's birthday. He thought Holly and I should reconcile.

"I didn't second guess you about your marriage," I'd told him. "Don't second guess me."

"We didn't have kids," Grady said.

"You think I'm happy about that? But for Frankie to see Holly and me like that, barely speaking, tension you could cut like wire, it was worse."

Mom used to say that Grady was born into adulthood, very sure of what he knew. Growing up, everything about him was so measured, so wise, so ordered, it made me want to scream. Maybe it got to Eileen, too.

"Frankie would have been all right," he said.

"Frankie?" I said. "He hears things that aren't there, has friends that don't exist. He's a sensitive kid. Divorce or not, I don't know if Frankie will be all right."

"Then help him. Encourage him to come out of his shell. Get him in the 4-H. That's a good group of kids."

I shoved the tongs I was holding right up to Grady's face. "Stay out of it. Just stay the hell out of it."

I knew then he had no idea, though just that week I'd laid out the truth to Holly, and she'd sworn to keep quiet until I was ready. I had loved her— still did—and I'd certainly been attracted to her. When we married she was pregnant, so I nudged doubt to my toes and took my place at her side. I'd hoped *husband* was who I was. But I was wearing a pair of boots made for other feet and the longer I wore them, the more they hurt. Holly didn't know what was wrong. It was more than just the bedroom stuff, though that grew dismal enough. I lost interest in us. I went to work every day and came home to something I didn't want. Here is the most cliched thing in the world, but it fits: I came home to a lie. There was no one thing that tipped us over in the end. I didn't hunker down in a duck blind with some guy who was more than a friend, or slink off to the bar in Shreveport that caters to the same-sex crowd. There were attractions, sure, but I never acted.

Holly was grateful to have a place to pin our troubles,

relieved to know it wasn't her, that she was innocent.

That she was hoodwinked.

"It wasn't my fault," she'd said.

"No," I said. "Not that."

I picked up the bucket rig and drove down Route 7 toward my father-in-law's place, where Grady would be waiting. I hadn't been out since Friday night, before the shuttle fell. At first, what I saw along the highway was normal landscape: lush fields, swampy spots and the branchless lower trunks of our towering pines, stark as charred asparagus. But a half-mile down the road, a pasture was littered. I could make out chunks of black and bits of white that looked like foam. A rod-like thing stuck out of the grass. For another mile I saw nothing odd, but just over the rise at Avitt Tindale's ranch, seven horse vans were parked in Avitt's front range. The riders were spread in a line, heads down, aiming for the thicket that bordered his place. I should have been searching, too. My own mother had lifted hot metal from the highway, before she knew she wasn't supposed to. Now, my son had done more.

I turned off the highway at 104, where two feet of blue tarp covered something that lay beside a wire fence. Next to it was a rustic cross, made from twigs. Acid rose from my gut like a vicious cloud; the orange juice dump had been a mistake.

A sheriff's deputy blocked the dirt road that led to Cloyd's place. When he signaled me past, I spotted Grady's car and a black SUV with government plates that I figured to be FBI. Frankie was across the grassy meadow holding the reins of his horse, letting Rosco graze with the bit in his mouth, which I'd taught him not to do. Signs of my absence hurt. Frankie spent Wednesday nights with me, and two weekends a month. Other people were filling the space I once took up in his world.

When Frankie waved, I rolled down the window and pointed to my mouth. He looped the reins over Rosco's neck and took off the bridle. When he looked back at me for approval, I gave him the okay. Frankie favored my mother—same gray eyes and the dark wavy hair of Lila MacFarland's youth. Funny how it would skip a generation like that. He gestured like her, too, and when he was talking about something he'd thought hard about, he would rub the side of his finger across the tip of his nose, a feminine gesture that made me nervous for him. Turns out it was nothing to worry about, and wasn't that typical. The things about Frankie that came into focus for me were so often the wrong ones.

Now Frankie was talking to Parris Parker, whose parents owned the place next to Cloyd's. I'd known Parris since high school but had never been around him much. He was only about a head taller than Frankie, with blond, short-cropped hair and, I could just see from here, a bald spot starting. I sat watching for a moment. Frankie was pointing into the Parkers' woods, probably in the direction of his find. My son was beautiful. What was going on in his head back then, I'll never know.

When I climbed out of the rig, Holly's father shook my hand, though I doubt he wanted to. "Ain't we got us a mess?" Cloyd said.

I nodded in Frankie's direction. "Should *he* be here?"

"He's already seen it. Can't go back now. It's that other one, Parker. Should he be here? Makes my butt itch, have a queer around."

It was useless to get on a soapbox. I was pretty sure Parris wasn't gay. "Parris is okay," I said. He'd left Frankie and was coming our way.

Cloyd shot me a stern look. "You got a boy to watch out for."

I let that one go, too, and I should not have. Frankie's head is on straight about things like that now, no thanks to his grandfather. But back then I worried about slippage, the low notions Frankie would pick up when I wasn't around. "Frankie is fine," I said.

"That boy is always alone," Cloyd said. He was keeping tabs on Parris as he talked. "Boy gets in the woods and just sits on some damn log he likes. If he's not smoking, what's he up to?" Holly had told me about the woods. It worried her that he was sitting out there more now than when we first split.

"It's been hard on Frankie," I said. "We have to let him deal with it best he can."

Parris was within earshot now. "Something ain't quite right," Cloyd said loudly. "Lot of things ain't right." He stalked off, passing Parris without so much as a nod.

With a patient smile, Parris watched him go. What his life was like in that town, for a man so different, I could only imagine. "Nice boy you have there," he said, and when he shook my hand it was plenty firm. Parris was fit, you might even say buff, but he didn't check me out the way gay men did. The mutt he had with him showed more interest in my ass. The dog was a birder of some kind, and it had found an irresistible odor on my shoe.

"Kids," I said. "Got to get out and look around. I think he was up at daylight, looking for stuff. Anything to get out of church."

"He was telling me about it," Parris said. "But he doesn't look at you when he talks, does he? Kind of looks past you."

"Frankie looks at me, no problem," I said. "It's just that he doesn't know you." The dog had followed his nose to a spot in the grass, but now he was back, snuffling around the heel of my boot.

"Maybe that's it." Parris cast a glance in Frankie's direction. "I bet the teachers like' him."

"He's mighty good with numbers. And he likes to read." In high school, Parris had been a smart kid, too—artistic, and a loner. He'd been best friends with Eddie Briesbecker, who died in a hunting accident over in Yellowpine just before we graduated. Parris never seemed to have anyone to hang around with after that.

"That tree where he found it," I said. "It's on your dad's property? I might have to take down a couple of trees to get the rig in there."

"Whatever you need. Technically the place is mine, too." Parris snapped his fingers and the dog bee-lined for the spot where he pointed. Nobody around Kiser trained their dogs like that. People think that small Southern towns treasure their eccentrics, but Kiser wasn't one of those storybook places. Parris owned a tile business and did pretty well, but when he refurbished his house in town, he painted a scene around his front door so bizarre that the neighbors complained. It was just animals, but they were bright and anatomically odd, like in a Picasso. "He'll tile your new house real good," Junior Pierce told me once. "But you wouldn't invite him to the housewarming."

"Good luck," Parris said. "Holler if you need help."

I hiked over to where Frankie stood with his arm draped over the pony's rump. Frankie got on well with animals. He wasn't anti-social; he had friends. I put my hand on my son's shoulder. "You okay?" I wanted to take him in my arms, but he no longer cared for hugs in front of strangers.

"I was just riding," Frankie said. "I was watching the ground. I heard something, like someone called my name. I looked up and there he was." He pulled a bit of mud from Rosco's tail. "Can I come with you and watch?" He turned to look at me, straight on.

"I'm not sure anyone should watch," I said. "You better stay here." When Frankie was little and he wanted something he couldn't have, we'd try to distract him. Now I nodded toward two men in dark windbreakers, standing by the SUV. "Those guys from the government?"

"Yeah. One's FBI. The other's an astronaut. He thanked me. It was cool."

"Awesome," I said. Normally Frankie would groan when I borrowed his lingo—back then the word was not so common—but this time he was silent. I put my hand on top of his head, tousled him a bit until he smiled. "What you hear is not really voices, is it?" I asked. "The way I'm talking to you now?"

Frankie looked across the meadow, into the trees. "It's kind of weird," he said. "You know how a thought comes to you? Like the answer to a question on a test. You know you don't know the answer. But something pops into your head, and it doesn't seem right and you don't know why you're putting it down. But it turns out it's right. I don't know. It's sort of like that."

My son had intuition, probably that was all. Maybe it spoke more clearly to him than to the rest of us. Or maybe he just listened better.

"Wish me luck," I said. I put out my fist and he knocked his against it. It was the guy-to-guy send-off he favored in those days.

I headed for the edge of the clearing where Grady was waiting for me. Behind him the trees rose in unadorned splendor. I thought the hardwood forests were beautiful in winter, with the foliage on the ground, and above, the branching miracles of cellulose and lignin. Over our heads the sweet gum balls hung like black jewels. The ash leaves that had stayed through frost were drained of color, brittle and defiant. They rattled in the breeze that had come up. I wondered what my boy might hear in the movement of those stubborn leaves.

Grady looked tired. My brother had a good poker face for disaster, but on the local news last night he'd seemed beaten. All day, people had been calling in reports of human remains. It was Grady's job to guide the government types down dirt paths and logging roads, to find out if the caller had spotted an astronaut's arm or the disconnected tibia of an unfortunate heifer.

"How're you holding up?" I asked.

"Thought you might be away this weekend." Grady's voice was hoarse; I could tell he'd had no sleep. It looked like he hadn't shaved since Friday. "I figured Houston," he said.

"Got this sore throat," I said, "so I didn't go." I'd been spending a few weekends in Houston, without explaining why. I figured my best shot at some kind of honest life was to move to the city and hope nobody in Frankie's world would hear anything more about me.

Grady ran a hand across his eyes and pressed on his temples. "You got a girlfriend there or something?"

I didn't answer right away. In Houston those weekends I would wander the streets, walking past the clubs, wondering if I wanted a part of what happened inside. What would life be like with no one watching? Turned out it was nice. It wasn't long after this day that I moved. It's been seven years now; things have worked out.

"No," I said finally.

Grady didn't look convinced. "Because if you do," he said, "you just need to say so. Frankie, he thinks it's because of him. He thinks the whole thing is because of him. It's how kids do. And he's more insecure than most."

"Did he tell you that? Did he tell you we split up because of him?"

"You know he gets that look, like he's not even here. He's checked out and gone somewhere else. Where's he gone, Wes? What's up with that?"

"So he daydreams. It won't hurt him. His grades are good."

"Holly says he's bored senseless in that school," Grady said. "Right out of his gourd."

"Let's just get to work," I said. I never would have asked Grady to take my place in Frankie's life, or help fill the gap when I left town. I'd hoped he would, it just didn't turn out that way.

I followed my brother into the brambles, through brush with vines so tough they'd trap a horse's legs. Grady held a head-high briar aside for me—the kind we called a blanket-shredder, with inch-long thorns that could ruin an eye. "Look up," he said. "Over your head, two o'clock." What I saw was an orange suit with a leg dangling out of it, as though the fabric had been ripped away. When we got closer, I could see there was no foot at the end of the leg. The torso was cradled by two branches in a deep crook, about sixty feet up. The astronaut's pose was awkward, but the arms of the tulip tree had received him with dignity, above the eager sniff of scavengers. He still had his helmet on, and I gave thanks that no one had to look around for that, maybe with his head inside.

"None of them burned," Grady said, gazing up, shading his bleary eyes from the sun that poked through for a moment. "Not a body part so far."

The skin of the dangling leg was dark, we could see that from where we stood. "African-American," I said.

43

Grady nodded. "Michael Kirkland. Payload specialist. Somebody found the foot by a mailbox yesterday." He rubbed his face with his hands. "Can you get the rig in here?"

I looked around for a path. The trees were thick. "Over there," I said. "We take down that sweet gum, I can squeeze through between those two beeches."

"I know you hate this," Grady said.

"Why me?" I said. "Chandler's got a bucket truck. You know how I am."

"I could go up instead."

"There's insurance rules. Nobody goes in the bucket who doesn't work for Horton."

"If it helps any, there's no one else I trust this much."

"To do this?"

"Yeah. And not to jaw about it." He tipped his head in the vague direction of the black SUV. "They don't want this in the newspaper. That deputy you passed out at the road, he'll keep the media out. Not forever, though."

"Cecil Dawson, wasn't it?"

Grady shrugged. It was Dawson who'd taken my brother to lunch last month, the day after the Kiwanis met to pick a high school queen for the Piney Woods Festival. At the meeting, Grady had pushed for Vanessa Johnson, a five-foot-eight beauty with brains and grace. But the Kiwanis said they weren't ready for a young woman with nut-brown skin to lead their parade down Main Street and sit with the mayor at the Saturday barbecue. Grady had delivered a tongue-lashing: Half the town's school was

African-American—get over it. At lunch the next day, Dawson leaned over his plate of green beans and baked chicken and said sourly, "We thought you were one of us."

I eyeballed the distance between Michael Kirkland and the ground. "What if I get up there and puke?"

"You won't. Think about the mechanics. It's an object you have to get out of a tree, a puzzle you have to work out. He might be stiff."

"Christ. I hadn't thought."

"Do what you have to do. He can't feel anything and the NASA guys, they just want him down. You don't have to tell anybody how it happens."

I got the chain saw out of the rig. The tree I needed to take down was only about twenty years old. Sweet gum wood isn't much good for carving but the bark is deeply ridged, which makes it handsome, I think. I made my quick cuts, and when the tree had fallen, I gave thanks I knew how to do something in life. Better than what was to come—today, next week, next year.

I moved the bucket truck into position and climbed in, setting the chain saw in its usual spot, as if this were an ordinary day, where I might have a water bottle stashed in the corner. I could have used one now. Adrenaline had shooed the NyQuil fog, but dread had left my chest heavy and my throat hurting more. I pulled the lever and started to climb. When Frankie was five, I'd broken the rules and taken him up. He could barely see over the top of the box and I could tell he was apprehensive. As we started to move, he grabbed for my pants leg. I put his other hand on top of mine, on the controls. "You see," I said, "we're a team." Some of the apprehension left his face and he looked into the sky, where he must have thought we were headed. "Higher, Daddy," he said. Soon, he let go of my jeans, and my heart sank a little.

The tree that held Michael Kirkland was already showing the bumps of first bud. Tulip poplars go bare early in fall, are among the first to green up in March. I think of them as bullish, optimistic trees. Their tough wood made good canoes for the Indians. This one had broken long ago, and two branches had grown together to make one. Inside the new branch would be a layer of bark, an inclusion where cells would have knit themselves together into a woodworker's treasure of swirls and iridescences. A tree will always try to heal itself. The forest floors are full of death, but the trees themselves, they breathe life and claim it. A boy could be drawn to that, couldn't he? Frankie made good grades in those boring classrooms. He had secrets he shared with no one. At twilight he went into the woods and sat on a log. What was wrong with that? The living trees spoke to my son; the dead ones spoke to me.

I needed to take out one big branch to get closer to my charge. Reaching for my chain saw, I looked down at my life—my heroic brother just below me, and at the edge of the meadow, my beautiful son. As far as I knew they still loved me, in their innocence of who I was, of who I was about to become. My son looked up to me, and my brother trusted me. I was living on borrowed time. I was not yet, to them, infested with rot.

The chain saw ripped through the interfering branch and it tumbled to the ground. I moved the bucket closer to the astronaut's body. The smell was sharp, but not yet foul. In the dark tint of his face shield, I saw a reflection from above, the jagged end of a limb that did not survive his fall. The crows had been on him; there were droppings on his chest. If only, I thought. If only this were the hardest thing. I reached around Michael Kirkland's waist and pulled him toward me. He wasn't stiff. Inside his suit, broken bones bent him in the wrong places. I laid him as best I could across the box, and held on for the journey down.

I like the texture of bark, the feel of wood in my hands, the staunchness of a tree that is connected and enduring. In a piece of wood a man can sense the forbearance of all that has come before, and the juice of this earth, with a sensuality not unlike lust. I craved a man with such steadiness, though it would be years before I realized it.

The man I live with now is grounded and true. Ben is sitting with me today, at the doctor's office, as we prepare for the moment when Frankie arrives to live with us, when we begin his long journey back, through therapy, maybe to college, out of the depths of what has been troubling him. When he wrecked Holly's car there was alcohol in his system, but not enough to have caused such a loss of control. He says he passed out, and maybe he did, but we believe he might have aimed the car at a tree. The psychologist here is one of the best in Houston for treating this sort of thing. Ben has a good income and we will do whatever it takes. I expect the doctor will ask about our family, about my life with Frankie. If she is a patient woman, which I suspect she is, I will tell her a story.

Though I've carved many pieces of wood since leaving Kiser, I have never touched the spalted oak. If it spoke to me, I wasn't listening. Out of the mysterious and complex scars of a tree, a woodworker is obliged to create. From a wound, beauty rises.

# AGAINST THE SKY

The Saturday morning the space shuttle broke apart and spread its shatter from Dallas to Shreveport, Gabriel Dixon should have been hauling short wood on Ernest Oteen's bobtail truck. But the truck had broken down again and needed a carburetor they'd have to send to up to Eno to get, so Gabe was frying bacon over his stove's last working burner when the crashing boom arrived and the kitchen window threatened to rattle right out of its frame. Gabe froze, fork in hand, as the roar pounded on for one merciless second after another, pommeling his eardrums with a mighty wrath, burring every cell of him until he shuddered as keenly as the walls. The egg he'd set out met the floor with a splat he could not hear, but he reached out in time to catch his plate before it, too, doddered off the table.

The train of thunder faded, and Gabe looked out his back door to see three plumes of smoke waggling across the sky. The sound on his TV hadn't worked for months, but he turned it on anyway and saw a grim newscaster and a group portrait of the astronauts, all smiles before their launch. The camera shifted to an empty landing strip and families being hustled into a bus. Gabe dropped into his sofa with the weight of what he'd seen in the sky. The old cushion rose up around him like a bulwark.

When the phone rang, it was Raymond, the son he could not be prouder of, who was driving down from Fort Sill this weekend and bringing with him a woman he claimed a seriousness about. Raymond hadn't said much on the subject of her; Gabe had a suspicion she was white.

"Hey, Pop. You hear it?"

"Sound like a pipeline exploding," Gabe said. "These walls been shaking."

"TV says debris was falling everywhere. All kinds of stuff, all over the place."

Gabe stretched the phone cord until he could see out his front window, through the plastic he'd taped up for warmth. "Big piece of something, like some kind of foam, right in my yard, by the street."

"Maybe a tile, or piece of insulation."

"You still coming tomorrow?"

"Be there about two." Raymond lowered his voice a notch. "Pop, something you need to know about Denise."

"You going to tell me she's white."

"It's not what you think."

"What do I think?"

"That there's nothing else to it."

"You be with who you want," Gabe said. "No matter to me. Though your mama, she would have been unhappy. But don't be bringing her here if you're ashamed of us."

"Her people aren't rich."

"No, I don't guess they are."

After they hung up, Gabe went back to the kitchen and sat down at the table to finish his toast. Ants had found a crumb from last night's sandwich. His foot found a sticky spot on the floor, under his chair, where he'd cleaned up the egg. He despised this floor, a yellowed vinyl with streaks that once might have been red. Alma's stroke had come while she was on her hands and knees washing what would never look clean. He used to tell her, *don't*. But that day, two years ago, he was shooting dice with Peego Godett and Hershel Brown. He wasn't here to say *don't*.

Now Gabe searched out the back window for pieces of this new catastrophe. The yard was mostly dirt, a few patches of weeds. In front of a dilapidated shed was a rusted charcoal grill and a wood pile, next to a lonely bush of some kind. A chicken wire fence was falling over the plot that Alma had favored for butter beans and squash. When Raymond was little, he used to follow Alma around and beg her to let him help. "Okay, Little Man," she'd say, "put me some seed in this row. Careful now." He would set in a seed, then do something funny, like spit on it, or sing it a lullaby. "Why you do that, Little Man?" Alma would say. "You're sure a silly farmer."

Raymond would cry out then in his little-boy pitch. "No, Mama. I'm a *crazy* farmer." It was a joke between them, silly or crazy. They were always laughing, those two.

Gabe put his dishes in the sink, checked the chicken he was thawing in the refrigerator and turned on the oven. Into a big pot he dumped two cans of beans, along with three jalapenos, which was as many as he could stand and probably not enough for Raymond. He wondered what the girlfriend liked. Raymond had said they'd stay for dinner but they wouldn't stay the night. That was a pronouncement Gabe could have predicted. His son sent him money every month, but he'd rarely been back home to Kiser in the six years since he'd joined up. At eighteen, Raymond had been a six-foot-two specimen of honest, naive vigor the U.S. Army knew just how to use. Now he was a staff sergeant, a veteran of Kosovo, and George Bush was rattling his saber for Iraq. There were so many ways to lose a boy.

Gabe got down on his hands and knees and gave the nasty floor a good scrub, wedging a rag under the short leg that made the table rock. The kitchen was in order, but the rest of the house needed cleaning. He started in the bathroom. He couldn't fix the hot water faucet that was corroded shut, but he scoured the basin and polished the scummy fixtures. When the beans were done, he hiked over to Ernest Oteen's to see if he could line up any work.

The next morning, Gabe was swabbing a greasy layer of dust from the front window sill when a patrol car pulled up. He watched Cecil Dawson put on his gloves, inspect the foam without touching it and stake a generous triangle of yellow crime tape around it. Dawson was a big man with a reputation for zealous enforcement. Last fall, seven fretful months after 9/11, he had brought the fairgrounds rodeo to a halt after finding an untended box with a suspicious white powder on top. He'd taken over the public address system and asked people to evacuate, but when the volunteer firefighters opened the box, all they found was one of Sara Farnsworth's prize-winning pound cakes with confectioner's sugar sprinkled on it.

Now Dawson was at Gabe's front door, knocking harder than he needed. The two times Gabe had been picked up for being drunk and disorderly, Dawson had been the one to do it. Gabe shoved a half-empty liquor bottle under the beat-up sofa. He had not yet had a drink this morning. He wanted to go this whole day without hooch so the white girlfriend wouldn't get a bad impression. Dawson knocked again and Gabe limped to the door. One leg was considerably shorter than the other. He'd been the youngest of nine and doctors were a last resort.

Dawson pointed toward the piece of foam. "Looks like something from the space shuttle. The U.S. government wants all the pieces back. Somebody's got to make sure they don't get tampered with. I'm asking you to do this. I mean sit your butt right out here and watch it. Can you do that?"

Gabe nodded.

"Don't know when someone'll be here to pick it up. We got us a disaster." He was scribbling on a clipboard; his car radio car crackled with urgent voices. "Get your coat. Let me see you out here so I can move on."

Gabe didn't know if he had a choice. "Be out in a minute," he said. He found the fleecy Cowboys sweatshirt Raymond had sent him, and topped it off with his ancient blue parka. Next to the TV was a little American flag that Alma had bought when Raymond packed off for boot camp. Gabe stuck the flag in his pocket and carried his kitchen chair outside, where Dawson was pacing. The chair fit on a bare-earth spot next to the yellow tape.

"Federal offense to touch this stuff," Dawson said. "So don't. Don't let nobody touch it." The deputy's radio squawked again; in the distance there were sirens.

"Won't no one get near it," Gabe said. Dawson gave him and the crime tape a last once-over. The way Gabe figured it, Cecil Dawson had no call to be so puffed up. The man had seen trouble, just like everybody. His son had come back from Desert Storm with the Gulf sickness. For a while, after his discharge, the boy had worked part-time at the post office. He was pale, tired-looking all the time, and when he sold you a stamp he was slow in making change. He hadn't worked there long. Maybe now he didn't work anywhere.

Dawson squeezed into his car, turned on the flasher and drove off to manage his disaster. Gabe took out the American flag, set it inside the triangle of crime tape and pulled up his hood. It looked like he wouldn't be doing any more house cleaning. Already his nose was running from the cold. Inside the parka's deep pocket he felt for a handkerchief. His fingers touched a mangled tissue, and a pint left over from another day. The bottle probably had a few swallows in it, but he left it there. He wiped his nose on the tissue and settled into the chair to take in the Sunday morning quiet of his neighborhood. Polktown was a cluster of cinder block and wood houses, mostly ignored by the white folks in Kiser, unless one of its inhabitants ventured two blocks west toward Main Street to buy, say, a tube of toothpaste at Carson's Drugs or a can of ant spray at Frick Brothers. Gabe had done just that last week. As usual, the hardware clerk had followed him around, plucking invisible litter from the floor, asking if he needed help.

When a worn-out muffler broke the peace, Gabe straightened up in his chair and saw Peego Godett cruising toward him in his Chevy Blazer. Peego was wearing the usual pristine Fedora on his balding head and a pair of expensive sunglasses he liked to squire around in. He had owned up to selling weed, but the market in Chireno County was good for meth, so chances were he'd graduated long ago.

Peego rolled down a window and stuck out his skinny face. He had a new soul patch on his chin. "What's this?" he said. "You do some crime with this piece of Styrofoam?"

"Piece of the shuttle."

Peego whistled. "You think so?" He climbed out of the SUV and walked to the tape.

"Wasn't there Friday night is all I know," Gabe said. "Space ship come down, there it is. Can't nobody touch it."

Peego put his hand out to the foam. "Says who?"

"Hey!" Gabe pushed himself out of the chair, waving his arms. "Leave it be. I don't want no trouble."

"Okay, okay." Peego drew back. "Might be radioactive, anyway. So why you out here?"

"Police ask me to watch it. That deputy, Dawson, he come by here."

"You be sitting out here in the cold 'cause Poundcake ask you? You a fool, Gabby-o. Space a white man's playground. Man on the moon, what for?"

"They been organizing people to search for pieces."

"Hershel Brown, he say he got a piece on his roof."

"They been searching for bodies, too. One a black man. Michael something."

"A space brother?" Peego snorted. He craned his neck to see in the back yard. "I believe I take some of that firewood you got back there."

Gabe straightened the little American flag, which had fallen in the breeze. It needed an anchor. "Be pretty damp. You got to dry it out."

"That's all right. I take five pieces."

"Cost you five bucks."

"You forgetting you owe me." Peego started toward the back yard. "And it ain't worth but three."

"Okay. Long as you give me the credit."

Gabe fiddled with the flag a bit more. If he popped it out of its plastic stand he could stick the flag pole right in the ground. He twisted the pole until it came free and poked it into the earth, close to the foam.

From in back of the house, Peego let out a yelp, then a string of expletives. He came around the house in a hurry, sunglasses low on his nose, like he'd been looking over them. "You got a big fucking problem at that wood pile."

"Told you that wood too wet."

"No man, bigger than that. You got a hand next to your wood pile. A fucking hand. Off a some dead person."

"What do you mean? You jacked up on something."

"It be laying there in the dirt. And it's off of some fucking white lady."

"You telling me I got a white lady's hand in my wood pile?"

"That's what I say."

Gabe didn't see anyone coming, so he left his post and followed Peego to the wood pile. There beside it was indeed a woman's hand. Five fingers and most of a left hand had been shorn off just above the wrist. Not a bone was broken. It lay there palm up, slender fingers touching, the thumb falling delicately across the palm. A green fly crawled over a gold band on the ring finger. Gabe's legs went weak; he thought he might gag.

Peego squatted to get a closer look. Some kind of gray beetle was creeping across the wrist. "You think it's off an astronaut?"

"One of them was a white lady." Gabe leaned a little over the hand, hoping his stomach would hold. "Shit, man. What we going to do now?" There was no blood. It was the palest piece of flesh he'd ever seen, bony and drawn on the top, swollen on the bottom. The thumbnail was filed into a perfect oval shape. "Best give me your phone," he said. "You got service on that new thing?"

"No way, motherfucker. You not calling no fucking police on my phone. You call Deputy Dawg, use your own fucking phone."

Gabe waved a hand to shoo the fly. "Lord, we got to cover this. And we ought to say a prayer."

Peego was picking through the wood pile for the biggest logs. "I believe it too late."

"Never too late. I bet she's got some kids." Gabe bent his head and said a prayer to himself. Peego tossed three fat logs aside.

"We got to cover this," Gabe said. "Might be there's a plastic bag in the house. I'll go see."

When Gabe returned, Peego already had piled one load of wood in the Blazer and was headed back for another. "Three more dollars," Gabe said, and held out a Sav-A-Lot bag. "Here. Put this over top. Anchor it good with some logs. I believe I'll go back in and call."

A crow had landed on the wood pile. Peego took the bag and waved it until the bird flew off. "I see you later," he said. "After you do your goody-goody thing."

When Gabe finally got through to the 911 dispatcher, she sounded stressed. She put him on hold for what seemed a long time. While he was waiting, Gabe heard helicopters overhead and remembered the families on TV being ushered into the bus: a teenage boy and the pretty blond wives, one holding a toddler in her arms. A wave of ill feeling came over him about the whole sad mess.

After the dispatcher took his information, Gabe walked back out and sat beside the crime tape. His neighbors were coming home from church, and the street was starting to stir. Polktown was not the sorry poor of the projects south of town. Gabe's neighbors tried, most of them, and worked at whatever they could get hired for. They held their heads up and tried to raise their children right, though a good many of the young ones strayed. Alma had taken Raymond every Sunday for worship and study at True Cross Gospel Church, and he'd escaped the biggest troubles. He was handsome and his skin was light. It had got him some things.

The woman who stepped out of Raymond's car that afternoon was a little on the thick side, but proportioned. Her dark red hair fanned out in a frizzy triangle that ended just below her ears. Gabe would not have called her beautiful, yet there was a grace about her movements as she reached inside the car for her purse, lay the strap over her shoulder and gently closed the door. A cell phone and a pack of cigarettes stuck out of a little pocket in the quilted jacket that tightened at her hips. She turned and smiled nervously in Gabe's direction as Raymond came around the car and put his arm around her. Her face looked kind, but Gabe had expected more glamour, a woman who gave off heat.

Denise put out her hand. "Raymond's told me so much about you," she said.

Gabe couldn't remember when he might have last

shaken a white woman's hand. Hers was warm, despite the cold, and there was a delicate feel to the bones, the way they felt more malleable than a man's, as though they could adapt to the task at hand—a caress of a chin or a bicep, for instance. If her hand were to fall to the ground, the thumb might languish across the palm in the same slender curve as the hand in his back yard, yet there was a bit of roughness to her skin. Gabe wondered if Raymond got a charge out of the contrast between his color and hers, as they lay next to each other.

"Only one lane open on 91," Raymond said. "Debris everywhere." He described the litter on both sides of the highway—small pieces that looked like gray metal, something tall and white, like a cupboard. His grammar was careful, the ends of his words claiming space in the air. Gabe had heard this exactness before, when Raymond returned from being stationed in Germany. "He don't talk like us," Alma had said in the bedroom one night. "Should we be happy or sad?" She was mending one of Raymond's shirts, where a buttonhole had frayed.

"Raymond, he's a man of the world now," Gabe had said. "Things going to be different."

Alma had knotted the black thread thoughtfully and snipped it with the sharp little scissors her grandmother had given her. "Long as he come home," she said, so quietly Gabe had strained to hear. She spread the shirt on the bed and fingered its foreign label. "Ever so often, he got to come home."

Now, Raymond nodded in the direction of the crime tape. "What's with this?"

Gabe explained about Dawson's visit. "We got more debris out back. You don't want to be looking at that." When he described the scene at the wood pile, Denise's mouth dropped open. "My Lord," she said. "How awful for you."

"I got a bag over it, good and snug. Dispatcher say they coming out and pick it up soon as they can. So I be guarding front and back, too."

"Kind of unbelievable," Raymond said. "You'd think it'd all be burned."

"And they were almost home," Denise said. "Almost to Florida." For a moment, no one spoke. A flock of noisy geese passed overhead.

"Hey, look here." Raymond popped the trunk of the car. "We brought you something." Inside the trunk was a big square box that said Sony.

"It has a twenty-seven-inch screen," Denise said. "We bought my mom one just like it."

Gabe touched the edge of the box. "This for me?" He ran his finger over the bar code, that mystery price tag. "You shouldn't be spending your hard-earn money like this."

"Wait'll you see the picture," Raymond said. "You watch the Masters, it'll be the greenest green you ever saw."

Gabe smiled and gave the box an affectionate slap. "My man Tiger, he going to burn it up." He put out his arms and Raymond enveloped him in a hug. Gabe could feel Raymond's hip was against the top of the pint in his pocket. When he pulled back, Raymond's wristwatch caught some of the old parka's ratty threads. They had a laugh over that. "You too good to your old dad," Gabe said.

"Nah." Raymond pulled a last blue thread out of his watchband. "If Denise'll open the front door, we can get this puppy inside. Feels like it's going to rain." He watched Denise's backside as she walked up the porch, which Gabe took for a lustful gesture until Raymond turned to him with a dark look.

"You've been drinking already," Raymond said.

"Ain't had a nip, not even to keep warm."

"Not today. Please."

"It's not but just a little bit in this bottle and I ain't touched it. You hook up that TV, find Denise something to watch. Stay inside where it's warm. Everything going to be all right."

"I'm asking you, Pop. Not today." Raymond hoisted the TV and shouldered past him.

After Denise held the door, she walked to the car where Gabe still stood. He'd hoped they would both stay inside, so he could sit in his chair alone. This day with no drink was taking its toll.

"I almost forgot," Denise said. "I made you something." She pulled a tote bag out of the back seat. It was green and blue, with a big logo on it: Save the Earth. Two loaves of bread were sticking out of the bag. "I hope you like whole wheat. I'm trying to eat healthy."

Gabe had planned to fry up the chicken for dinner. Eating healthy was something the folks on Main Street might do, but in Polktown, folks ate what was cheap. "It looks real good," he said. "I surely do thank you."

She set the tote bag on the ground and took a cigarette from her pocket. "Do you mind? If I smoke?" Gabe shrugged, watching her light up. There was a small hump in her nose, not too noticeable at first, but certainly there upon close examination, like the small round ears in Alma's family which had passed themselves on to Raymond. Gabe wondered if Raymond would end up father to a light-skinned, small-eared baby with a hump in its nose.

"Raymond's been good to me," she said. "My son Nathan, he adores him. He runs to the door when Raymond comes over. One day Raymond took him fishing. They had a real good time. He's six, Nathan is. He's with his father this weekend."

Gabe felt his eyebrows rise, but clamped them back down. He didn't want to show surprise at this revelation, a child already in the picture. He didn't want her to realize how little he knew about her, how little Raymond shared about his life. "Raymond, he loved to fish," he said. "Used to take him out to Minden Lake. One time he caught this big old catfish. Raymond just a little thing, maybe five. Thought that catfish going to drag him back into the lake. He wouldn't let me help him no way. Finally, he get that catfish reeled in. He's so proud. He see this white lady with a camera taking pictures of her grandkids. He calls out to her and ask would she take his picture, too, with that big fish. I tell him, don't you be bothering that lady.

63

But she do it, says she happy to. I give her the address, but we never get the picture."

"Maybe the picture didn't come out." She took a big inhale from her cigarette.

"That might be it." Gabe reached for a bottle cap that lay by his feet. The yard was littered with pop tops, candy wrappers and a flattened can of Mountain Dew.

Denise lifted her foot and crushed the half-smoked cigarette on the heel of her clog. "I really don't smoke very much. Just certain times." She picked up the butt and held it between her fingers.

Gabe had offered her none of his usual courtly gestures. He hadn't opened the car door, he hadn't offered to take the tote bag from her, nor did he now rush to find a place for her cigarette. It was his experience that white folks approached the space around them with a sense of expansion. His long-standing habit, when he was with them, was to stay in his own space and guard it. He considered now that Denise seemed like a perfectly nice person who might have many good qualities, and he didn't want her around in any kind of permanent way.

A gust of wind came up, and Denise shivered. "Go on in," Gabe said. "See how Raymond's doing with the TV." He picked up the Mountain Dew can and a wrinkled end of paper that had covered a straw.

"You're okay out here?" Denise asked.

Gabe nodded. She cupped her hand around the cigarette butt and carried it into the house.

***

By the time Raymond had hooked up the TV, Gabe's street was buzzing and his front yard was full of white folks. Norris Tibbet had driven up in his black hearse, which prompted the three little Morris boys across the street to come outside. They would have crept closer had they known that the crisp-moving, square-jawed man who climbed out of Dawson's squad car was astronaut Charles Bradley.

Tibbet carried a white body bag under his arm. Mud stained the fancy stitching of his cowboy boots and the pants of his undertaker's suit were shredded at the ankles.

"You been in the briars," said Dawson.

"Showing my respect," Tibbet said. "Ruining some suits. It don't matter."

Bradley peered at the object inside the yellow crime tape. "Not ours," he said. He reached into the triangle and turned over the foam. In the corner was a sticker that said Home Depot. A smile flickered above the astronaut's prominent jaw. "Hey," he said, "could have been." Gabe watched the color come into Dawson's face and thought if it weren't that Dawson had it in for so many people, Gabe might have felt sorry for him. Bradley showed more mercy. "Better to be safe," he said, and clapped the deputy on the back.

Gabe led the men to the back side of the house. Behind him he could hear Dawson's handcuffs, clipped to his belt, rattling under his jacket. The first time Dawson had arrested him, the night that Raymond phoned with the news he was leaving for Kosovo, Gabe was so jagged he could barely stand. Dawson had put his hand on Gabe's head and guided him into the cruiser's back seat. The second time, a month after Alma died, Gabe was involved in a shouting match after a pool game at Munk's Grill. Dawson used the bracelets then. When the cuffs clacked shut and lay hard against Gabe's bones, he had begun to sweat, despite the cold night. His legs felt heavy, as though they, too, were bound.

Raymond came out the back door and met them at the wood pile. Dawson struggled to type their location into the GPS. It looked like he's never used one.

"I find the other yesterday," Gabe said. "Peego find this one this morning. Wish I seen it yesterday, too, so's I could cover it."

Tibbett smoothed on a pair of latex gloves and knelt down. Gabe's stomach was hurting and he didn't want to look at the hand again, so he moved behind Tibbett and focused on the top of his bent head. The undertaker had combed a few hairs over a bald spot in that self-conscious way that white men did. The bare spot was pinkish; Gabe could see blue veins showing through.

Bradley glanced at the hand, then set his gaze on the horizon. "It's Jackie," he said. He put a thumb to the back of his neck and rubbed. Clouds had gathered and it was starting to sprinkle.

Dawson unzipped the body bag a short ways, and that narrow opening, for such a small bit of human flesh, struck Gabe as the saddest thing yet. Tibbett put the hand gently inside, peeled off his gloves and rose stiffly to his feet. "Let us pray," he said, and waited for the others to assume a reverent pose. He recited the familiar psalm about green pastures, motioning for everyone to join in. Gabe had not been much of a church-goer; he wasn't sure of the words. Finally it was over. "Oh, gracious God," said Tibbett. "We commend to You the spirit of Jacqueline Dietz. May she remain in Thy eternal rest."

Bradley crossed himself like a Catholic and recited a prayer Gabe had never heard. "God bless the children," Gabe said quietly. Tibbett folded the ends of the body bag to make a triangular package. He led Bradley and Dawson in a procession toward the hearse, carrying the package in front of him like a platter of grief. Gabe hung back, picking up the Save-A-Lot bag and turning it inside out without touching the side that had rested on the hand. Raymond stood nearby, running the fingers of his left hand over the side of his head. Gabe knew that meant he was itching to say something. His son wore no hat; other climates had toughened him.

"That lizard Peego," Raymond said. "What was he doing here?"

"He get some firewood is all. He don't cause no trouble." Gabe squashed the Sav-A-Lot bag until it was as flat as he could make it and pushed it into a pocket.

Raymond looked hard at his father. "You doing business with him?"

"No, I ain't doing no business with him. What makes you think I do?" Gabe took a few steps back, reached into his other pocket and took out the pint. All of his muscles were hurting and there was a fuzziness between him and the rest of the world. The big knot in his stomach threatened to double him over.

A raindrop trickled down the side of Raymond's head and slipped behind a small round ear. "You're a mess," he said, before he turned on his heel and stalked off. Gabe watched him go. His shaky fingers closed around the bottle cap and for the second time today he thought he might puke. He considered how many hours had passed since his last swig, how many hours were left to go. As soon as Raymond disappeared around the house, Gabe hurled the bottle against the cinder block foundation. The sound of shattering glass broke through his cotton brain and sent a pain across his forehead.

Gabe walked slowly to the front yard, where Bradley met him and put out his hand, thanking him for his help. Dawson had taken down the crime tape, leaving Gabe's flag to stand sentry over the disgraced foam. Across the street, the knot of onlookers now included Jasper Whitehead and his boom box, which prompted the wiggly Morris boys to dance. Tibbett started up the hearse. After Bradley climbed in, Jacqueline Dietz's hand was carried away to the throb of a rap tune.

When they were gone, Gabe went inside and joined Raymond on the sofa in front of the TV, placing himself over a ripped spot in the green fabric where the foam cushion showed through. Raymond seemed calmer, so Gabe pointed to the remote. "Show me what this baby can do." Raymond went through the controls methodically, coolly. Gabe asked questions, and Raymond answered them.

There wasn't any friendly patter. Denise stood by the TV, dusting bits of packing off its edges. She'd stuck a ball cap on her head to ward off the rain; hair fanned out from it in stiff abundance. "I might use your bathroom," she said.

"Down the hall, babe," Raymond said. "There's a hook for the door. Won't stay shut otherwise." He turned to Gabe. "Is there any toilet paper?"

Gabe rocked back in the sofa so hard the frame creaked. He threw up his hands. "This ain't no goddamn barn. It's the home you grew up in."

Raymond made a scoffing noise through his teeth. "Just look at this place. It's falling down. You don't pick up the trash in the yard, you don't keep up with what needs fixing. When Mama was alive, things got done. And no lowlife like Peego Godett would dare show his face around here."

"You got a lot to say on a subject you don't know jack about. What's with the way you talking, all uptight like? You at home now. You with family."

"You going to tell me I'm talking white? Is that what you're saying?"

"I ain't saying. Just telling you what I hear."

"Shit. Peego Godett, of all people. Maybe you understand if I say it like you said to me: You be with who you want, it don't matter to me. But Mama, she would have been unhappy."

Gabe faced his son square on. His eyebrows formed a hard line across his forehead, where the shooting pain had turned into a dull ache. "Your mama, she cut folk some slack. Your mama believed a man innocent unless some-body prove he not."

"Peego's done plenty. He ducked the time."

"Not talking Peego."

Raymond narrowed his eyes in a severe way Gabe had never seen. "You're right," he said. "Mama cut folk a lot of slack. And here's something I didn't ever tell you. The day she died, she knows you not at work like you supposed to be."

"You watch yourself now. Don't be saying."

"They come looking for you," Raymond said. "She's telling me that on the phone. She fix dinner for you and you don't ever show up. You over at Alfonso's, shooting dice, doing shit, drinking, I don't know."

"You don't know. That just it. You don't know."

"I know Mama scrubbing the floor because she so mad at you. You don't do what you say you going to do." Raymond started to say something more, then stopped. Gabe knew what it was. Raymond blamed him for her dying.

"I hear it—you mad," Gabe said. "But you got no right to be talking to me that way."

"I got a right because it's the truth."

Gabe looked hard into Raymond's eyes, where he saw he could never measure up. "Truth is, you always been telling her why you can't come home." He picked up a sofa pillow, one that Alma had made, and fingered the worn edge. She would get low-spirited sometimes, after Raymond joined up. She knew what she needed and Gabe couldn't give it to her. "You come here thinking I live like the hogs, that I'm selling drugs. You out there with your arms all folded, judge and jury. You don't know nothing about my life. You never around. You make good in the Army and I'm proud of you as I can be. You got a whole big life and you out there living it. But now you come around with the redhead."

"I knew it. I goddamn knew it." Raymond tossed the remote to a table and stood up. "You're such a fool."

Gabe hissed. "What is it with her anyway?"

"You know what it is? I'll tell you what it is. I can depend on her."

"You fucking with me, right? That's what you think? Then you the fool, son. You the fool."

Denise had come out of the bathroom and stood now at the edge of the room. "Get your things," Raymond said, and stood up. "We're leaving."

"Raymond, don't," Denise said.

"Sure," Gabe said. "You go ahead and leave. Just like you always do." He grabbed the remote and started fiddling with it.

Raymond was at the door. "We're leaving. Now."

Denise picked up her purse. "I'm sorry," she said. Gabe waved the remote in a circle over his head, dismissing them both.


Gabe reached for the half-empty Seagram's bottle he'd shoved under the sofa and let himself have three swallows. With Denise and Raymond gone it didn't really matter, but he couldn't think where he had any bottles now except this one. Nudging it back under the sofa he turned on the TV. There was just the one station he could get without cable, a station from Shreveport. It was showing the five o'clock news, with scenes from the Chireno County VFW, which had turned into a feeding center for search volunteers that had come from all over. The color was truly bright. He felt the liquor reach the fuzzy edge of his brain.

A white lady was talking to the TV reporter. "How we going to feed all these people?" She was making biscuits in the VFW's little kitchen; flour dusted her apron and spread over her arms. "There must be three hundred people in this place already and more's coming. I bought the last sack of flour at Brookshire's. They were out of meat by noon. My husband drove over to Nacogdoches to buy some things, but they got their own crowd there. Ain't enough grocery stores and restaurants around here to feed this many people three times a day. Anybody's got some food, bring it on down."

Gabe went into the kitchen and lifted his big frying pan off its nail. He took the chicken out of the refrigerator and gave the pieces a good coating with all the flour he had left. When the pieces were fried up, he piled them onto his largest dinner plate, covered them with a clean towel, and slipped the mound sideways into a paper bag. He found his parka, which had left a damp spot on the sofa, and reached to take one more swallow from the bottle. A new thought struck him. It seemed now, in this moment, he had to be bad in order to do good, and maybe it had always been that way.

Wedging Denise's bread loaves under his arm, he carried everything outside, where it was raining hard and nearly dark. Only one wiper on the old pickup worked, but he could see well enough. He drove slowly through town and turned on Route 7. The VFW was three miles north, just past the fairgrounds.

The parking lot was full of cars, plus a ten-wheeler from the National Guard. Gabe found a spot in the corner next to someone's new Lincoln. Outside the door, two white men in plaid shirts huddled with their cigarettes. When Gabe peeped in, he recognized the BINGO banner from the TV pictures. The place burst with people and noise. His was the only black face.

A woman with silver hair piled stiff on her head came over to him. "What have you got there?"

"I got this chicken," he said. "Weren't nobody to eat it."

"Your wife cook it?"

"No m'am, I fry it myself. Still nice and hot." He remembered the spicy beans he'd left at home. It was stingy not to bring them.

"Well, bless you," the woman said. "Put it on that table over there, where the people are lined up." She took the loaves from under his arm. "I'll slice these up," she said, and smiled at him the way white folks do when they see a black man doing something they approve of, like coming out of church, or pushing a baby carriage. Gabe set his baby on the table and uncovered it.

The line of hungry searchers moved slowly along the table. Right off, a man reached for a breast from the bottom of Gabe's pile. "You bring this? Think I could eat every piece." He was about twenty-five, with a thin scratch under one eye. A gold cross hung over the T-shirt he wore under a flannel shirt. Another man picked up a leg. His yellow hair was plastered to his forehead; a slicker over his arm was muddied and torn. "We're mighty grateful," he said to Gabe.

The two men settled at a table nearby. Their teeth broke the chicken's golden crust and steam poured out of the flesh. Grease made their pale fingers shine. Gabe hoped the searchers would find as much of Jacqueline Dietz as there was to scoop up. Everything was out there, under one big sky. He reached into his pocket and touched the wad of plastic that had covered her hand.

The stiff-haired lady returned and set the bread slices beside the chicken, which was disappearing fast. "There," she said, spreading the slices into a perfect fan. "Like my mama would say, made with love." She gave Gabe another one of her smiles.

Gabe nodded. "Your mama, she know." Alma had told him white women were lax about washing their hands after they used the toilet in public restrooms. He hoped this lady wasn't one of those. He took a piece of Denise's bread in his hand. The texture was thick and the taste was strong, almost sour. The bite he took was too big. Struggling to chew, he looked across the room and saw Dawson coming his way, gloves clutched in one hand like a bouquet of leather fingers. Just behind him was another deputy, the skinny one with glasses, Carl Hubble.

"The ring," Dawson said when he got close. "Where is it?" He was looking at Gabe.

Gabe wasn't sure he'd heard right. He pushed the chewy mass of bread aside with his tongue. "What ring?" he managed.

"It's her left hand," Dawson said. "She wore a wedding ring." People nearby had stopped talking and heads were turning.

Gabe tried swallowing the bread, but it was having a hard time going down. "I didn't see no ring," he said. His words came out muffled. He maneuvered some of the bread into his cheek, which bowled out like a plug of tobacco was stuck in it. Just then he figured something out about the hand. His debt to Peego was paid.

Dawson was flapping the gloves into his palm, marking time. He had not been out of the rain long enough to dry off, and a few big drops rolled around on the brim of his big deputy hat. "If you give it to me now, there won't be no trouble."

Gabe swallowed the rest of the hindering bread. His fingers had closed into a fist, so he stuck that hand into his pocket. "I'm saying it weren't no ring on her hand." Dawson was boring a hole in him. His face was hard, and he looked more haggard than this morning.

Inside his pocket, Gabe felt the plastic bag, a heroine's shroud. He should never have come. His chest was starting to hurt, as though the bread had stuck there. He looked away, across the room, where Dawson's son had just come through the door. He was walking with a cane, carrying a bag of groceries. Dawson saw him, too, and for an instant his eyes were visited by a tender sadness. Gabe wondered what it was like to give a son to the Army like that, a boy never to be himself again. All around were the other fathers, the ones whose sons were whole.

"I believe I'll go on home now," Gabe said. He thought he'd better hurry. He grabbed for the empty chicken plate, but the edge of it was so greasy it flew out of his hand and whacked Carl Hubble on the shin.

"What the hell," Dawson said.

"It slip right out of my hand," Gabe said. He bent down to get the plate. As he straightened up Dawson reached for his arm.

"You been drinking," Dawson said. "You better come with me."

Gabe backed away. "I'm not going with you. I ain't done nothing." His eyes found the short route to the door. In two seconds he'd decided, and took off in the fastest seesaw motion he could manage. Pain shot through his short leg and into his spine. As he scuttled past the stiff-haired lady, her hands flew to her chest, as if she'd seen a mouse. He gripped the plate tighter.

Outside, the rain came in waves that drove sideways as Gabe gimped through the parking lot. He looked over his shoulder but didn't see Dawson following. The pavement was full of low places. Water sloshed over his sneakers, soaking through the shoelace holes. When he scrambled into the pickup, rain blew in and splattered the seat. Gabe crouched down in the cab, more to think than to hide. The rain was roaring. His breath was coming hard, the nerves in his bad leg were on fire, and some new torture spread across his lower back. He was afraid to drive away. If Dawson thought he'd been drinking, he'd set him up for the DUI. Raindrops ran down his face. He could not focus, to think what to do now. He felt under the seat for an old towel he liked to keep there, and found another pint of Seagram's. This one was three-fourths full. He took the bottle to his lips and drank until it was half empty. Then he sank back in the seat and closed his eyes. The pain in his gut began to ease while the nerves in his back relaxed, as though he'd stepped into a warm bath. Outside, the noisy rain came in sheets, but the darkness of his closed lids offered comfort. He saw in his mind's eye the hand of Jacqueline Dietz. He heard the zipper of the body bag go its short distance. What a sorry piece he was and would always be.

Gabe sat up and searched the parking lot, all around among the cars. He didn't see Dawson or anyone else, so he started the engine and rolled slowly to the road. Raymond was out there somewhere, under the sky. The windshield wiper had only one speed and it was sorely tested, but he followed the edge of the two-lane as best he could. Up ahead, along the shoulder, the phone lines wobbled in the wind and rain.

# A CAMP IN THE WOODS

My brother, on his deathbed, could not get out of his mind the big things he'd screwed up in his life. Each would nag at him for a day or so until he seemed to come to terms with it, then he'd move on to some other mismanaged affair. Carl believed he'd mistreated his first wife, which he had, and he fretted that he'd ignored our aging father, which was also true. There was one event Carl never mentioned, though, and I wonder if he thought of it at all. The incident with Plato Winchester has troubled me more and more over the years. Perhaps at the end of my life, I will have to answer for both of us.

People used to say about Plato Winchester that you could drop him in the woods buck naked and hungry, and if you went back in a week you'd find him fully clothed and well-fed. He was a throwback to another time, a woodsman who could sling a gut hook and skinner with the grace of a TV chef filleting a trout. We thought of him as a modern-day Davy Crockett, though his life—as we knew it, anyway—lacked mythic proportions. Plato was not a romantic figure. His social wits were on the dull side and near as we could tell, he'd never had a woman's company for more than a night. Diabetic, Ghandi-thin and prone to mood swings, he lived deep in the woods in a broken-down camper with nothing for company but his private thoughts and a posse of hog dogs. He came to town once a month for his pills, and when he did, people who didn't know him cut him a wide berth. His beard was longer than the one you imagine for Methuselah and his clothes were holey and rough. A couple of times a year, to raise what little cash he needed, he'd sell off some boar that the dogs had hunted. Though he fed those Plotts and curs from the pet food aisle in the grocery store, Plato would leave Brookshire's with nothing for himself but a can or two of beans. He named the dogs according to the alphabet, like tropical storms. The yellow cur he carried in his arms that winter was number sixteen, a young one he called Pip.

It was a Saturday just before Christmas, the year after 9/11, when a few of us were standing around in Frick Brothers Hardware, as we often did, hiding from the honey-do lists back home. I remember quite well that

Teeter Minkins was there, and Junior Pierce and my brother, Carl. We had known each other for a decade or more, and had fallen into a ribbing that was predictable but sharp. There were jokes about my thinning hair, Teeter's big soft gut, the colored toothpicks Junior stuck in his mouth when he was trying not to smoke. Carl was the biggest needler among us. He was a sheriff's deputy, and down there at the jail they made innuendo a high art. Junior was complaining about the three-day trip he was about to make to Dallas, a town he hated, when Carl interrupted him. "There you go again, leaving that good-looking wife of yours alone on a Saturday night. I got a mind to give her a call." Nobody said anything. It was an old joke of Carl's that he should have dropped, once the rumors started about Claudia.

Just then Plato came through the door, looking to buy some nails. He was building a lean-to. We were surprised he wasn't whittling his own pegs.

Right off, Carl started in. Lately, he'd been leading us into new territory and that day he must have had a bee up his ass. My brother was an angry man, a boiling kettle with a tight lid. Once, I'd tried to talk him into meditating. I did it myself for a couple of years. "Lay off me, Jimmy," Carl warned. He preferred to drink beer and pick at people.

Plato was an easy target. "Well, if it ain't society's dropout," Carl said. "Wearing the same damn shirt as last time he come in. What corpse you steal it off of, anyway?"

"Man don't need but two shirts," Plato said. "Short-sleeve and long." He showed a lot of teeth when he talked,

and they looked to be in good shape for the kind of life
he led. We figured him to be pushing sixty. Teeter, whose
wife was diabetic, predicted someday Plato's body would
turn on him. Kidney, eyes or heart, it was just a matter of
time.

Carl waved a hand in front of his nose. "The shirt needs
a washing. Unless that puppy of yours got the farts."

Teeter made a harrumphing sound from deep in his
flabby chest. "When a dog cuts the cheese," he said, "it
don't smell like B.O."

"A healthy dog don't fart," said Junior. "Ain't that
true, Plato?"

"Anything that eats will fart," Plato said. "Thing that
smells around here is Carl." His voice was squeaky and
high, which we figured was the price of not using it much.
He counted out some quarters for the nails and picked his
young cur up from the floor. She nibbled at his beard. "I
got things to do," Plato said. "Not like you flapjaws." He
never hung around long for our kind of fun. He wouldn't
have understood our jokes, anyway. Plato never read
a newspaper and the radio in his truck didn't work. He
kept his own counsel and kept to his beliefs, whatever they
were. His life was admirable in its way.

And we were a shameful lot.

After that December morning, we didn't see Plato again
until February, just after the space shuttle came apart.
NASA had asked people to go into their yards and look
for debris. There was a number to call if you found something, and plenty of warnings about leaving everything

right where it was, until somebody official could pick it up.

Five days into the mess, Plato showed up at Bostic's and said he had some shuttle parts in his pickup—bits of metal, pieces of foam, something he said looked like glass. Our group was in the store, warming up after a morning of searching in the cold and damp, wishing Roy Bostic had put in that coffee machine he kept talking about. Carl was buying Excedrin to keep himself awake. He was punchy. With all the chaos and searching, he hadn't had much sleep.

"I brought in what pieces I could," Plato said. "Pip, she licked some, but I don't think she hurt nothing." Through the window we could see Plato's three dark Plotts scrambling around in the truck bed, tongues hanging out. The yellow cur was crawling on the steering wheel. "There's eleven pieces," he said. "One was still warm when I picked it up. I'm fixing to take them to the sheriff's."

Carl put one hand on the counter and the other on his hip. I had a feeling there was a piece of conniving working its way around his brain. "Well now," he said. "That presents a problem."

"I thought they were wanting it all back," Plato said.

"Oh, they want it back all right. Trouble is, you weren't supposed to touch it." Carl looked full of himself, as he sometimes was with his deputy duties. He liked to take a man and turn him on his head, figuratively speaking. When Plato wasn't looking, he winked at us, then at Roy. We should have stopped him, I know we should. "All this stuff is dangerous," Carl said. "Probably radioactive. We're going to have to confiscate your truck, and the dogs, too."

The look on Plato's face was one of surprise, but also defiance. The kind of man he was, he didn't much believe in rules. "You're not doing that," he said. "You ain't taking my dogs."

"Got to do it. For everybody's protection. And you've got to go over to Shreveport and get tested at the hospital."

Teeter was struggling to hold back that giggly laugh he had. Junior had turned his head away; I thought he might explode. Roy ducked into the back of the store; he didn't want any part of this. When Carl got started, there was no stopping him. He had his deputy game-face on, all serious. Teeter looked over at me with his fist to his mouth. We knew we were in for a humdinger.

"The thing is," Carl said, "you probably took in so much radiation you might have only two weeks to live."

I remember thinking then, he's gone too far. I remember thinking, too, this is a hoot, one for the books.

"You're not taking my dogs," Plato said. There was a flash in his eyes. You'd think he'd have been speechless with the shock of it all. Instead, he was circling the wagons around life as he knew it.

Carl raised his voice. "Didn't you hear me? You probably got only two weeks to live."

Plato crept backwards toward the door. "Not my dogs." He was turning red in the face.

"Well," Carl said, "then you go on to the emergency room. They'll know what to do. Better take the dogs with you. I bet they can test them, too."

"Now Carl," I said.

"I'm not going to no hospital," Plato said. He headed for the door, but stopped long enough to say one more thing, the thing that made this story the fun it was to tell the whole next day. Turning around, he squared up and faced us.

"If I've got only two weeks to live, I'm going to spend it hunting hog." Then he bolted.

We all pretty much dissolved at this point, but I knew I better go get him. It wouldn't take him long to get away.

He already had the engine running so I banged on the window. When he rolled it down I saw a pleated lamp-shade on the seat beside him. The oddity of that stuck with me.

"It was a joke," I said. "You don't have anything to worry about."

I thought Plato might blow his stack, but he just sat there for a moment, like he was recalculating everything he'd known up 'til now. The yellow cur was in his lap, licking on the steering wheel. "Okay, Jimmy," he said. "Okay." He stroked the cur's neck. "Vulpecula and Anser."

I had no idea what he was talking about. "Carl gets carried away," I said.

Plato held up his hand. A jagged scratch ran along the outside of his pinkie. "One of them pieces cut me. I put it here under the seat where the dogs can't get at it."

"I wouldn't worry about it," I said. "But you could go to the hospital and get checked out if you want. Get a teta-nus shot or something."

"They doing those tests like Carl said?"

"No. He made it all up. I swear."

Carl and Teeter had come outside and were congratulating themselves. "Should have seen the look on your face," Teeter said.

"You had me going," Plato said.

"I ought to make you put every piece right back where you found it," Carl said. "The NASA people, they wanted to know where everything landed. They wanted to map it all, pick it up themselves. You better take it to them. There's some of them set up over at the fairgrounds." He pulled a Marlboro from its pack and lit it.

I suppose each time Carl reached for a cigarette, his psyche perked up and his healthy cells groaned, as if one part of the body was at war with another. My brother had smoked since he was fourteen, a pack a day for much of his adult life. He wasn't the first of us Hubbles to die that way. He told me once, toward the end, that he'd been expecting it. I knew if he could have quit, he would have. There was no mystery about his death. His lungs couldn't take the abuse, no matter how much his brain might have wanted to live.

I know there are people who think emotions stick in our tissues, giving off signals that change the workings of the body. I think about the body's misfires, messages that get sent and can't be taken back, like words you wish you'd never let out. Carl and his first wife, Suzanne, had terrible fights—vicious rows, and him with his sharp tongue. He did damage he could never repair, not to her, not to him.

None of us know the forces at play within us. We see men who die from grief, and men who refuse to die, hanging on for dear life well past the time their doctors predicted they'd leave us. Day after day, sometimes year after year, their brains decline to hear the message that time is up. Maybe the brain catches hold of an idea and can't let it go, no matter the physical evidence that contradicts it. What do any of us know about how the end truly comes about.

Plato never showed up at the fairgrounds to hand over his shuttle debris. When we found this out two days later, Teeter, Junior, Carl and I drove out to his camp in the south tip of the county. We thought maybe he hadn't understood, or he thought Carl was joking about that part, too.

We discovered him propped against a tree, as though he'd just sat down to take a rest. The yellow pup was at his side. Doc Meadows couldn't find a cause for his death— no insulin shock, no kidney disease, no heart attack. Plato would not have left his dogs willingly. "Sometimes people just die," Doc said. "The body is a mystery."

I would argue that the body isn't all of the mystery, that there are parts of the mind the Almighty has drawn a veil around, at least for us mortals, at least so far. I believe in the spirit, in the connection between mind and body, and I believe if a man makes up his mind to live, he improves his chances against all odds. It helps if a man can know the lay of his land—if his cells are dividing when they shouldn't, or if his heart is tired and needs a rest. My cardiologist, a man I've known all my life, has been frank with me about how much time I have left. Jimmy, he said, get things tidied up before Thanksgiving. Yesterday, I found a home for Plato's yellow cur, who's lived nearly all her eight years with me. I'm divorced now and my kids are grown. When I'm gone, Pip will have a new family, one that knows her story, and ours, too.

I hope my subconscious believes something different from what the doctor told me. I hope it can pull me through a little while longer, into February, on to spring. Of the four of us jokers who were in Bostic's store when Plato brought in what he'd found, I'm the only one still alive. If it leaves me holding the bag, then so be it. I am prepared to answer.

I never figured out the meaning of the lampshade in Plato's truck. But among the constellations, Vulpecula is a fox, and Anser is a goose.

# COTTONWOOD STAND

I t was mid-morning in early April, the sun high enough already to sweat up the brow of A.T. Sparks as he stood beside the roasting pig, his pleasure on this festive day dampened by worry and sorrow. A hundred of his kin were gathered at the old home place, and he was trying to focus on what was here and let go of what was not. The weather, though dry for crops, was decent for a family reunion and this year's turnout was particularly good. Just now, Billy Sparks was sitting on a picnic table, tuning his cheap guitar. Soon, the family would collect around him, hoping he'd practiced a new song since last year's dim offerings. Chances were he hadn't, and they'd go on as usual, pretending he could sing. It didn't matter; ritual thickened the blood.

A.T. watched his older son, the one with the money sense, baste the pig in strokes so precise that the boy—long since a man—might have been painting a mural. He knew that in a few years when Trevor's meticulous hands took over Sparks Heating & Air, and A.T. went fishing every day like a retired man should, that the business would thrive. Just look at the way the boy held the brush, lightly between two fingers, like a pencil, no sauce dripping to the coals, none of it wasted. Even in this small endeavor Trevor was efficient.

A.T. removed his raffia hat, a fancy one that Trevor had bought him, and swept its brim over two yellow jackets that were dogging the sauce jar. They were thick as thieves this year.

"I guess maybe you know," A.T. said, "I told your brother not to come. I've had it with him. He better mind his p's and q's from now on, because this family is done protecting him." In February his younger son, the one who could repair anything he had a mind to, had propositioned a teenage girl while he was supposed to be fixing a heat pump. If A.T. had known the girl was alone in the house, he wouldn't have sent Newnie over there.

Trevor set the basting brush in the sauce jar and covered it with foil. "There's something else, Dad. Something I've been wanting to tell you." His face had the seriousness that drew his pale brows low over his eyes. He was a head taller than A.T. and had a strong-jawed, Nordic look that would serve him well in the business. "I think Newnie's got his hand in the till."

"You got proof?"

"I'll get it."

A.T. scanned across the grass until he found his wife, wiping down the picnic tables. "We fire him," he said, "it'll kill your mother." Moira was a stout, good-hearted woman who'd raised two sons as best she could and cared for them with every fiber in her. Three months after they'd adopted Trevor, she finally got pregnant. The natural boy had been trouble from the get-go, a difficult child to love.

"People don't trust him," Trevor said. "They don't want him in their house."

"Then maybe," A.T. replied, "we got no choice."

For as long as he could remember in his adult life, Newland Sparks had kept a catalog in his head of women he knew, a Playboy stash of possibilities. He liked to sort them by their most appealing attributes: the A list for ass, the B list for breasts—whichever quality was most desirable to him. The lists weren't static; they needed constant tending. A woman could move to the top of a list if he spotted a tempting shape in her he hadn't seen before. A looker could move to the bottom of a list, or off altogether, if she started wearing frumpy clothes or put on too many pounds.

Suzanne Vickers, whose kitchen he stood in now, was a B-list girl. She looked like she was about a 38C, plenty to fill up a big hand. She'd called this morning to say the air conditioning wasn't working right. It was only the first Friday in April, but nobody wanted to be without air come late spring in Kiser. The temperature outside was already eighty.

"If we don't get on it now," Newland said, "you won't have any air by next week. That compressor's on its last legs." Tomorrow was Saturday. Since he'd been uninvited to the family reunion, he might as well work. Suzanne motioned for him to sit at the kitchen table, where she'd aimed a big fan, and now she was fixing him a glass of iced tea. He didn't know Suzanne well; she worked part-time in the insurance office where his wife kept the books. She was married to a first-rate asshole.

"Kyle isn't going to like this," Suzanne said. "It'd be better if he was home."

"When's he getting back?"

"I don't know. Sunday, maybe. He left yesterday to go hunting over Rockland way." She had her back turned, but Newland felt something he couldn't quite put his finger on. He figured the marriage wasn't all that happy. Kyle had a temper, and he'd been in a few scrapes. He had lost a couple of jobs, too, and now he worked for a logging outfit up in Eno.

Suzanne handed Newland the tea, and he made sure his fingers brushed hers. The baby she'd had in her first marriage—to that jerk of a deputy Carl Hubble—had tipped her to the heavy side, but she still had proportions. He took in the way her hips swelled under her shorts. "Why don't you go on and call up Kyle and talk it over," he said. "I'm sure he'd like to come home to a cool house."

Suzanne sat down and lit a cigarette. Her eyes looked tired, but her light brown hair was shiny and soft-looking, as though she'd just washed it and dried it in the sun. Newland wanted to put his nose in that hair, right there at the nape of her neck. Women liked him. He had the dark good looks of the best of the Sparks clan—straight black hair, brown eyes with flecks of gray, skin that tanned quickly in summer. He was not heavyset, as the Sparks men tended to be, nor did he have the weak Sparks chin. Below his thin lips was an appealing cleft.

"Teresa doing okay?" Suzanne asked. "Seemed like the other day she was coming down with something." A gray cat had come into the kitchen. Suzanne put down her cigarette and reached to pick it up. "How much for today?"

"Teresa's got a cold. Stayed home today. Didn't even wake up when I left. You paying cash or check?"

"Cash, if I've got it. How much?"

"Normally seventy-five for this kind of service call, but I can give it to you for seventy if you don't tell nobody." A service call was actually sixty. While Suzanne went to get the money, Newland made out a receipt. Later he would tear up the carbon and give Trevor a different one. He was good with the signatures.

When his cell phone rang and he saw it was Teresa, he figured she was going to ask him to stop at the store for something. "I just wanted to see how you are," she said. "Make sure you're not coming down with this cold." She said she appreciated him leaving breakfast out for her. She was playing real nice.

"You need anything?" he asked. They had a truce now; he could be nice back to her. Last year she'd stepped out on him, but they'd gotten past that. Teresa was a hard woman when you got right down to it. People just didn't know. She was pretty, sure, but she had a mouth on her. When she had one of her hissy fits, she'd imitate Newland and his speech problem. He had trouble with his r's. Once, when she had been smart about something, he'd slapped her. Afterwards, she threatened to leave him, so he apologized and begged her not to. She said she'd stay if he let her have one thing. Anything, he said. He'd been sitting at the kitchen table, like he was now at Suzanne's. She brought her leg up and kicked him in the ribs. I wanted to give you that, she said. You're lucky it wasn't your balls.

"There's nothing I need from the store," Teresa said. "No family reunion, I don't have to bother with all that potato salad." She finished with the usual complaints about his family, their blustery numbers. Newland thought of his mother, fanning herself on the porch of the dogtrot house his great-grandfather had built. A ring of cottonwoods hugged one side of the house. Fenimore Sparks had brought them down from Missouri because he liked their fluff and the soft rattle of their leaves. Tomorrow, under those trees, six picnic tables would be covered with food—the green Jell-O mold Newland hated, the homemade pickles he loved. The old washtub would be filled with ice and Coca-Colas. His mother would set out her special pecan pie.

Suzanne came back in the room with a blue envelope. "That Teresa? Let me talk to her." Newland held out the phone in his palm, so her hand would fall on top of his when she grabbed it. Her pink nails grazed his skin. Suzanne listened with her head down, then she said into the phone, "It'll all work out." Now she looked up and smiled at Newland. He sensed that she liked this, Teresa on the phone, the two of them alone together. She knew Teresa. She knew what he put up with. "Okay," she said to Teresa. "I'll let you know."

The kitchen was heating up. A sweaty spot had appeared between Suzanne's breasts, above the low neckline of her black tank. She had a gold chain around her neck, with a small heart dangling from it. Above the chain was a purplish brown spot, a birthmark maybe. She opened the envelope and counted out the cash.

"I could come out in the morning, first thing," Newland said. "This has probably been worrying Kyle. Why not surprise him? Take a load off." She caught him looking at her chest. He was never embarrassed at this; women liked a compliment.

The cat started working around Suzanne's legs. "I don't know if we can afford this," she said. Newland knew they didn't have much money. Besides Suzanne's daughter, Kyle was supporting two kids from his first marriage. Teresa hadn't wanted children and that was fine with him. Life was cheaper that way.

"I see you been working on the kitchen," he said. "It's looking nice. What do you call that wall color?" He wanted to soften her up. His eyes rested on a gouge in one of the cabinets that had messed up the new paint.

"White linen. Though it looks yellow to me. You're seeing that spot Ally hit with one of her toys, right after we painted. Kids. It just doesn't pay to spruce up." The hole had been created with force, and it was too high for a child to reach. More likely Kyle had one of his tantrums.

Suzanne went over to the kitchen faucet, which was dripping, and pushed hard on the handle. "This old thing, I swear. So you got a helper on Saturdays? I heard the Howard boy was working for your daddy some."

"Not for this. I don't need a helper for this." He wanted to kiss her neck, right above that mark. She wanted it, too, he could tell. She was facing him now with her arms across her chest, but he knew she was just being coy. He would touch that spot someday. He would stroke it and kiss it and maybe later rub the tip of his dick across it. A strand of his sticky juice would moisten her skin. He got up and dumped his ice into the sink, like the house-broken husband he was not. When he put his glass on the counter his arm brushed hers. "Be by about eight thirty," he said. If he got here early, maybe she'd still be in her robe.

That night, with Teresa in bed before nine, Newland went into the family room and stretched out on the couch. On the radio they were playing a Jimmie Dale Gilmore song he liked, one that Billy Sparks ruined every year. *Sometimes you're the windshield, sometimes you're the bug.* Billy would sing it tomorrow, and people would applaud, no matter how bad it sounded. Newland had told Teresa they were skipping the reunion because A.T. was mad at him—something about work—and it would pass. She didn't ask any questions. That Thompson girl, the stupid bitch, had been wearing a halter top and falling half out of it. Imagine, a halter top in February. Soon as he saw her she went right on the B list. Turned out she was nothing but a cock-tease.

Newland got himself comfortable on the couch, and let his thoughts drift. There was plenty of time tonight for a good session. Over the years, he'd liked to picture himself as a photographer with a woman on the beach, ready for a photo shoot. He would see that her nails were painted bright, her pubic hair groomed, the hair on her head blown dry and spread across her shoulders, some of it falling toward her breasts. If her nipples were not naturally big and round, he would give her that kind with a makeup box of rosy pinks and browns. Lately, his fantasies had been changing. Yesterday he'd stopped in the park to catch up on some paperwork. He saw Wanda from over at the courthouse, walking on her lunch hour. He waved to her and she waved back, lifting her shapely, sleeveless arm. That got him started. This time, instead of a makeup box, he had a toolbox, and he did playful things with the tools, things that might leave a little mark on her here and there.

He thought now about holding Suzanne, maybe pressing her up against the refrigerator, the purplish spot on her neck just below his mouth. He would dig his fingers into her arm. His dick would be hard, and she would—what would she do? Would she squeal, would she cry? Maybe he'd wrap his fingers around her wrists. You're hurting me, she'd say, and he'd practically come, hearing her say that. Just thinking about it, well. Here was the C list. Now she was on it.

Vern's Grill was a cramped, rackety place with seven red booths— not a one free of rips—and a row of scarred-up Formica tables. The place was known more for gossip than the eggs and coffee that were cheap but not as tasty as most folks could get at home. A few of the regulars were part of the Sparks clan, and that meant on this first Saturday in April the crowd was a little thin. Vern himself was subbing for his young cashier, who'd just married a Sparks and was hoping her recipe for vinegar slaw would suit that gang.

Newland arrived early and headed for the corner booth where Bert Nichols and Cloyd Bentley were shooting the breeze over their grits and fried eggs. He had to stand over them a moment before Bert made room. Cloyd was talking about a big piece of metal that had been found in the pond off Turner Road. "Sounds like it's in that fishing hole next to the Sparks place," Bert said. "Newland, you seen it?"

The pond across the field from the old dogtrot house, hidden by the cottonwood trees. When Newland was little, A.T. had hung a tire swing from a cypress growing on the pond's edge. Trevor never liked the swing, but Newland spent hours on it, the creaky to-and-fro becoming, over time, something he needed, like water or air.

"Don't know nothing about it," Newland said.

"You ought to go out and look," Cloyd said. "Big black piece, kind of sharp, sticking out of the mud. Probably from the shuttle. Just what people said would happen, with this drought and all. All kind of stuff showing up now, been under water two years."

Newland reached to touch the waitress on the elbow as she passed. Theirs was the cute one, on the A list for sure, instead of the old crone with no sense of humor. "Hey, honey, how about some coffee here?" When she turned to him, Newland gave her a good gawk at the chest, where her T-shirt stretched across her breasts.

"So how come you're not at the reunion already?" Bert swabbed a piece of toast across his plate. For a skinny man he could pack it away. "Don't they start up early?"

Newland shrugged. "I know what they all look like. Teresa's got a cold. No use giving it to a hundred kissin' cousins."

The waitress set coffee in front of Newland and left without asking if he wanted to order. Maybe she was on the rag. Maybe she had a horny husband who was giving her the business all night. He moved her off the A list. Let her join the crone on the zero list, right next to Carter Bostic, the bitch. Her and that miserable store, his family had seen to the end of that. He picked up his steaming coffee and his scarred thumb felt the heat. Soon he would be at Suzanne's. She'd be in her robe and they would go from there. He'd press his hips against her belly and she'd feel how hard he was. Maybe he'd have her, right there in the kitchen. Maybe he'd turn her over on the table. Maybe he'd light up one of her cigarettes and touch it to her hand. Then she'd make some noise.

Suzanne Vickers sat on the floor of her kitchen, in front of the big rattling fan, on the spot where she'd landed when Kyle had taken his last swing at her this morning, before he called her a dumb fucking cunt and stormed out to his pickup. Her husband didn't usually hit her anywhere that would show, but she'd have a black eye this time, and her wrist was probably sprained. She turned the fan so it would blow on the side of her face where she should be putting the ice, right this minute. It seemed like Kyle couldn't go six weeks without getting his fists on her. Once she'd laid the cash into Newland's hand, she knew she had it coming.

And Newland would be here any minute.

"He'll make a pass at you," Teresa had said. "After what happened with the Thompson girl, I'm sure A.T.'s going to fire him. He thinks I don't know about that girl." Teresa wanted a divorce. Without Newland's family, he wasn't much use to her. He couldn't protect her from anything, he couldn't get her anything. "I can do better," she said.

Suzanne opened her robe a little, exposing the tiny rose tattoo on the top of her breast. She'd put it there for Kyle when they got engaged. Now she heard a truck drive up and the feist dogs next door started in with their barking. A door slammed, and she heard Newland's voice, telling the dogs to shut up. She picked up her cell phone and hit the number five. "He's here," she said, and hung up.

Outside, Newland had been relieved to see only Suzanne's car in the driveway. He had on a clean work shirt and a newish pair of jeans, and he'd chosen loafers instead of his work boots, which were hard to get off. He'd made sure his socks didn't have holes.

When there was no answer at the front door, Newland walked around back. The feist dogs raced along the fence next door, their crazed high pitch assaulting his ears. He raised his voice to them and they raised theirs back.

On the patio, a folding chair was overturned. Newland knocked on the screen door. Behind it, the inside door was not quite closed. He tried to see in the kitchen window, between the blinds. The dogs calmed down for a moment, and it was then that he thought he heard weeping. He debated, then pushed in the door.

"Suzanne?"

The kitchen was a wreck. Two chairs were upturned. Spoons, dishes and a blue mug were scattered across the floor. The refrigerator was dented; a frying pan lay at its feet. Suzanne was on the floor in a heap, holding her cell phone. Newland's wish had come true: She was wearing a short pink robe. It was part way open in the front, exposing her bra; he hoped it was the kind that hooked in front. The gray cat was at her knees, watching him. Suzanne seemed stunned, and didn't even make the effort to cover herself.

"Jesus," he said. "Who did this to you? Did Kyle do this?"

"He wanted some cash, and I gave you everything. It was my fault. He's never done it like this before."

"That shithead. Where's Ally? Where's your daughter?"

"With her grandparents. She's up in Eno."

There was a bruise forming on her face. Fucking Kyle, Newland thought. He'd ruined everything. He helped Suzanne into a chair. The robe was falling open; her tits were real comers, a rose tattoo high on the left one—such a delicate thing, alone in its sea of flesh. He wanted to brush his lips across her skin, cover the little rose with his tongue, take it between his teeth.

"I'm okay," Suzanne said.

"Where's Kyle now?"

"I don't know. He won't come back. Not today. He never does." She was holding her wrist in her lap. "I need some ice."

"Let me get it," Newland said.

"No," she said. "I need to move." He reached to help her up but she waved him off. "I can do it," she said. "I have to." When she leaned over to push up, he could see into the gape of her bra, almost down to one nipple, big and dark. She stood slowly and fumbled with the robe until it wrapped more closely around her. The rose disappeared from view.

Newland stood aside so she could make her way to the refrigerator. Something deep and old surged up in him. His thoughts traveled to the dogtrot house, the cottonwoods spreading their green against the sky. Billy Sparks would be sitting under them soon, picking on his beat-up guitar, a dozen kid cousins kicking around in front of him. The way Newland had it figured, by the time he got born into this world, his parents had given the best of themselves to a child whose light curly hair came from who-knew-where, but whose name was Alan Trevor Sparks III anyway. After that, one more boy was superfluous. He had known this before he could put words to it, by the time he was twelve, when he'd loved to watch the cottonwood fluff as it strayed across the pond. He would stand on the old tire swing, scanning the brownish murk below, the fat, scratchy rope in his hand and one bare foot stretched out, far as he could make it go. Again and again he would swing over the water, warm air stirring against his skin, until he saw the snakes just under the surface. Only then would he drop in.

Suzanne leaned against the refrigerator, holding an ice pack to her face. The gray cat was twining her ankles. On the refrigerator door was a child's drawing. Newland reached out to touch it. "Ally's?" he asked. He thought he could smell Suzanne's hair, a scent like flowers and freshly washed clothes. Suzanne turned to look at the drawing, a picture for mommy on her birthday, she said. It showed a blue house with a chimney where the door should be. A window floated in the air above the house and through the window, smoke billowed towards a sideways tree.

Newland moved toward her and felt the nip of Suzanne's ice pack. With a slight kick he pushed the cat away and placed his hands against the refrigerator, framing her shoulders. She faced him, tensing, her back against the blue house and its troubled window. The child was probably in kindergarten, that ruthless place. Newland lowered his arms, so Suzanne could not duck under them.

"Move," she said. She held up the ice pack, like a child with a rock.

"Hey, come on," he said. "I won't hurt you." A chill came from her face, where the ice had been. He put his nose to her soft hair. It didn't smell of flowers, it smelled like ammonia.

"You're crazy," she said.

He pressed against her until he could feel her B-list breasts flatten against his chest. He put his mouth on hers, working against her lips and closed teeth. When her mouth opened for an instant, as if she were about to speak, he ground into her, his tongue reaching for the back of her teeth, the roof of her mouth. She didn't make a sound. Where was the pleasure in this? His cock was on her belly, he could feel her flesh surround him. Behind her head, the child's picture tore from its tape. He moved until he found her hip bone, lowered himself until he got his dick against her pussy. He thought he smelled the musk of her. Prying the ice pack from her hand, he pitched it to the floor. His father was going to fire him; he had nothing to lose. He shoved her cold hand under the seam at his crotch. She did not try to move it. Jesus, was she going to help him? What would it take. He put her palm to his balls and held it. There. And there. He took hold of her other wrist, the one that was hurting. She gave a little cry. Jesus. Fuck. Here it was. Oh. The dark water washed over him. He did not hear the door when it opened.

# THE GROUND

"Here's something to remember," his father said. They were in the garage, where his grandfather kept a shop. In the corner a stack of moving boxes stood higher than Frankie's head. His mother was in the kitchen making macaroni and cheese. She'd been fixing his favorites all week. Last night it was spaghetti and meatballs, ice cream for dessert.

"You wear these thumb pads. You hear me? Or else you wear the glove."

His father had been in the garage every day this week when Frankie got home from fifth grade. Normally he would be working at the tree service, or at the apartment in town where he was staying. Today he had given Frankie a sharpening stone, a glove and a little bag of thumb pads. He was teaching him to sharpen a knife.

"Show me the duct tape thing," Frankie said.

"Okay, but the pads are easier." The father took the boy's thumb in his hand and wrapped it with the tape. "Put the sticky side out, first time around. Then wrap four or five layers the regular way. You don't get a sticky thumb that way." He produced a tiny can and dribbled oil from the can onto the sharpening stone. "This keeps the blade cool. If it gets too hot, it won't sharpen right."

Frankie watched his father draw the blade across the stone. He stood very still, like a deer, listening. This morning he'd heard the March rain move over the trees, its wall of sound, then whoosh and the brattle of wet leaves, beech and ash, locust and oak, from here to the Parkers' place, where he'd found the astronaut last month. So much he has heard. The bark as it sloughs off a trunk, the twitter of one lonely leaf, the quiet tears of his mother in her room at night, the crickets, the bullfrogs, the flies. The ants. The thump of an astronaut's heart, falling to the ground. He has heard what he has not wanted. He has heard his brain in disbelief, the thump of his own bewildered heart.

"I have to leave Sunday," his father said.

"Next Sunday?"

"This Sunday. And there's something I want you to remember."

"The thumb pads. I won't forget."

"I want you to remember that I don't have a choice."

"Why can't you stay?"

"Frankie, I can't. You'll understand some day. Your Mom and I, we can't."

The boy looked at the stack of boxes. They were labeled: tools, books, miscellaneous. An ordered retreat. They'd been stashed here last year, at the grandparents' house where Frankie and his mother lived now, because his father's apartment was so small. The apartment in Houston would be bigger. The boxes would go.

"Now you try. Bring the blade toward you, at an angle, like this. Ten or twenty degrees."

Frankie guessed at twenty degrees and drew the knife slowly across the stone. He has never told anyone: He heard the shuttle come apart.

"You want to watch how you draw the blade. It makes a difference. That's more than twenty degrees."

He tried again. The blade made a rasping noise.

"Good. That's good."

Yesterday his father had showed him how to gut a fish. The day before, they tied a fly. Something to learn every day, like cramming for a test.

"I heard a joke at school today. Want to hear it?"

"Pull the blade more slowly."

"A little kid went up to his grandpa and said, 'Grandpa, can you make a sound like a frog?' When the grandpa asked why, the kid said, 'Because daddy says when you croak we're all going to Disneyland.'"

"That's sick."

"Yeah. It's funny. I could tell you another." In their old house, from his bedroom, he had heard them in the kitchen: a fist on the table, the slam of a cabinet, a crash of metal into the sink.

"Is it sick?"

"Naw. What did the zero say to the eight?"

"I don't know, what?"

"Nice belt."

"I like that."

"It's not as funny."

They heard his mother calling, the way she did when they all lived in their house. "Five minutes," she said. "Supper in five minutes."

His father turned to wipe a spot of oil off the table. Frankie drew the blade once more across the stone, slowly, just as his father had shown him. If he had not kept secret what he had heard, the roar that frightened them all, his father would stay. He touched the smooth side of the blade to his thumb.

# PREVALENT WIND

Eve Shulman liked to say she landed at Chadwick Manor Senior Care as an accidental tern, blown inland by chance and wounded in a rainstorm. She was an articulate woman who appreciated a sprightly turn of phrase, especially if it was hers. Pauline noticed this right off about Eve, who carried a commanding—some would say demanding—presence, with a voice that came from deep in her chest and traveled easily across a room. Even the residents who were a little hard of hearing, like Pauline, had no trouble understanding.

Eve had arrived at Chadwick on a hot September day in a city-owned van from Nacogdoches. It was a special delivery, strings pulled, and Pauline watched with curiosity as Eve tipped the driver with a bill so large he looked twice before he buttoned it into his shirt pocket. At the dinner table that night it was clear to Pauline that Eve thought the rest of them were just East Texas country. Eve was from Virginia, which made Pauline think of foxhounds, tri-cornered hats and a long-ago run of presidents. Eve might as well have claimed her home was Newfoundland, as far away as the peacock airs of Richmond were from Kiser. She had a diamond that stuck high out from her finger like a nail working its way out of a plank. Her dyed auburn hair was trimmed to sharp points at her ears and there were expensive highlights at the top. Someone tended her well.

Eve told them she'd been in Nacogdoches to deliver a university talk on the fate of Chilean artists during the Pinochet years. She'd broken her hip in a fall on wet concrete stairs and when she got out of the hospital, there were no rehab beds in town. Her doctor's mother lived in Kiser, in one of the antebellum houses at the edge of town. The doctor thought Eve and his mother might get along, so he sent Eve to Chadwick for recovery. The mama soon jetted off on a Napa Valley wine tour. That left Pauline and a couple of residents who could still get around to entertain a woman who, except for a broken hip, was in good shape and still on the easy side of eighty. Her stay would be memorable, even for the elders prone to forget. Months after Eve left, when the Columbia blew apart and the remains of an Israeli astronaut were found near Chadwick, the abrupt arrival of the foreign astronaut—and the need to import a rabbi to attend him—prompted many at Chadwick to recall Eve Shulman, the only Jewish person they had ever known.

The first day Eve came with her walker to breakfast, she sat in Buddy Jackson's usual chair, at the tiny table where Buddy liked to be alone in the mornings. She had a book to lay out in front of her, the way people arranged themselves in city cafes. When Buddy waddled into the dining room he went right over to her, pointed his corpulent finger and said, "That's my chair. I always sit here by the window." Eve dropped her chin so she could look at him over her French eyewear. "Then you can have it when I leave," she said, and went back to buttering her biscuit.

Woodrow Sparks, sitting two tables over, was smitten at once. When he whispered to Pauline he used the word saucy. He'd been a lifetime smoker and had a bad heart, but he left his oxygen beside his chair and took Eve a jar of jam. "It's strawberry," he said. "There's grape jelly, too, if you'd rather." He introduced himself. "The biscuits are pretty good here."

Eve wiped a crumb from her lip and held out her hand. When Woodrow took it, he held it a beat too long, as was his habit with women. It looked to Pauline as if Eve was used to the attention. "I do like a little jam," Eve said. "My Lenny, he's the one who loves jelly. I like more texture." She declined his invitation to move. "I'm settled here. Maybe at lunch?"

At noon, Eve took the chair beside Woodrow, who put his napkin in his lap for once instead of shoving it under his chin. Eve gave them an earful about her Lenny. He was her second husband, a fairly recent one, and she said he would have been with her during her convalescence were it not that Her Majesty—his mother—was in a Maryland hospital, possibly breathing her last. Lenny was a retired physician with an interest in plant remedies; she'd met him on a flight to South America. Lenny was good at fixing things, Lenny was good with money. Lenny was not at all bothered by the small notoriety her expertise had brought her. He was proud of the book she'd published, an event her first husband had brushed aside. She'd retired from teaching at a women's college in Virginia, and she ran on about that, too, in her voice that carried. At dinner that night, and for many dinners after, there was more, more, more from Eve. When she revealed that Lenny had lost his hearing in one ear, people looked at each other and nodded. Perfect match.

They wouldn't have known Eve was Jewish if she hadn't told them. She was not, she pointed out, a very Jewish Jew. Her observance was light. She didn't care for organized atonement. She did not live a life steeped in Jewish culture. This was a disappointment to the staff at Chadwick, and some ignored the revelation. The staff had tended another Jewish lady once, one who grieved publicly that she could not get her latkes and matzo ball soup at Passover and her bagels and lox on weekends. The staff had never been able to find those things—this was before the Internet—and now they tried to make up for it by showering Jewish food on this new Jew, one who did not care.

Eve confided to Pauline—ungratefully, Pauline thought—that if she had to force down one more frozen Lender's bagel with Philadelphia Cream Cheese spread from somebody's shopping trip over to Shreveport, she would die. Eve liked to talk to Pauline in a conspiratorial tone, and from the start she'd treated Pauline as if they were confidantes, though the feeling was not mutual. "I was this close to making the Freedom Ride," Eve said, and laid it on thick about her liberal causes and how she gave money to the United Negro College Fund. "That so?" Pauline said. She was prone to caution. Eve's public sympathies did not make her a sister. Evenings when the TV news came on, Eve would shake her fist and take the Lord's name in vain in connection with the Republican party. It was the fall of 2002, mid-term for the second Bush in the White House, and the hawks were angling for a war. Every night Eve made a show with the fists. She would turn to Pauline and say, "Are you with me?" Pauline kept quiet. When she'd moved into Chadwick with the white folks, she made a promise never to speak of politics.

Pauline had not been the only dark-skinned resident at Chadwick when she arrived, but the other two were men and they did not live long. Pauline put it on her praying list to have a woman come. When Rose Benjamin showed up, it was as if a window had opened in a stale room, and Pauline took a long, deep breath. Rose believed she was here by God's grace. She'd worked many years for the mother of Eve's doctor. Arrangements had been made, and now she was at Chadwick instead of the county home.

Good for you, Pauline thought, and set about learning what there was to know about Rose. She found her quiet and pleasant enough, except in the way she was always pushing Jesus. Rose had belonged to the Soldiers of Faith Tabernacle west of town. They were practically holy rollers there. Rose asked Pauline if she'd accepted Jesus as her personal Savior. Pauline didn't believe she had to stand in front of a congregation and proclaim Jesus. She didn't believe in any showiness whatsoever beyond a good gospel choir and some words from the pulpit that made sense.

"You're having trouble with your hair," Pauline said, after they dispensed with the get-to-know-you's. Pauline retained the old beautician's habit of sizing up cuts and color. "It's all broken off," she said. "Looks like it's falling out. What you been using on it?" Rose told her. "No, no, no," Pauline said. "That's for white hair, that Head & Shoulders. Way too strong for black. You got dandruff? Use the shampoo I give you. Your hair'll come back."

The two women managed a kinship, though Pauline soon realized if they'd been out in the world, they might not have taken up. Rose had not read much, except in her bible. In Pauline's view, Rose was intelligent, but her brain was not expanded. She had heard of James Baldwin, but she had never read him. "There's something I want you to do," Pauline said, and handed her a book, dog-eared and taped, a few pages falling out. *The Fire Next Time*. "We could talk about it. After you read in there some."

The two of them were lucky, Pauline knew, to spend their days among the white folks, Rose with her walker on wheels and Pauline in a motorized wheelchair. Not that Chadwick Manor was fancy. It was a one-story brick, low and mean. "Chadwick Minor," Woodrow called it, built with money from Horace Chadwick and his siblings, a tax write-off in memory of their mother. The rooms had not been redecorated since the eighties. "A plague of mauve," Pauline complained. The wallpaper was peeling at the seams, which the other residents blithely ignored but Pauline would poke at when she was in a pique. Air freshener spurted from plastic jars in the electrical outlets. "It stinks like cheap bath salts," Rose said. "They think old people can't smell." Rose only said these things to Pauline. Around the others, Rose was selective. When she did speak, unless she was talking about Jesus, she was inclined to address the floor. Sometimes Pauline wanted to slap her.

The white residents at Chadwick were polite and friendly to the two black ladies, as Pauline had heard them described, but not much interested. Rose and Pauline stood out but were invisible at the same time. No one asked about their families or their lives before Chadwick. A few of the elders couldn't keep them straight, though Pauline was stout and Rose was scraggy thin. They'd both lived all their lives in Kiser, and there was history with some of the folks, but they never mentioned it.

And now here was Eve, exotic bird.

"Was your family Reform or Conservative?" Lila MacFarland, a volunteer who bounced in twice a week with a super-charged smile to keep the elders entertained, had taken a special interest in Eve, fascinated by her Jewishness, enchanted by her wealth of education. "I could never be Orthodox," said Lila, eyes ablaze in stagey merriment. "Could you?" Her brown hair muffed around her ears like fledgling feathers. Pauline could tell she did her own color. She should have used something brighter.

Lila wanted to know all about being Jewish, but she'd never asked about being black. Pauline could have told her. Pauline could have told Lila how her son, a hard-working, big-dreaming rapture of a boy, couldn't get a loan because Lila's husband wouldn't give him one. Richard MacFarland had not apologized, had not said his hands were tied by the policies at East Texas Bank and Trust. He just said no. At the time, Franklin had a job at Tyson's and no bad debt. His white friend Jason, who held the same job, got a house loan pretty as you please. Jason said Franklin must have been holding back on him, that there was something sketchy in his past. Jason was naive—a nice way to put it. He didn't want to see what was right in front of him. He was just like Woodrow, who'd run up credit at Bostic's store whenever he conveniently forgot his wallet. Truman Wally, an elder at Pauline's church, couldn't get a little credit from that couple no matter how many odd jobs he did for them, no matter how many times he fixed their truck.

Pauline had forgiven, but she had not forgotten. She and Rose were the old peeling paper on the walls of Kiser. When the white folks at Chadwick started making over the Jewish lady, asking all their questions, Pauline thought something might change. Maybe their world was opening up. Maybe they would turn to Rose and Pauline and say, what about you?

Pauline put the slice of watermelon she'd been served onto Eve's plate.

"Full of lycopenes," Eve said. "You don't want it?"

Pauline shook her head. She never ate watermelon in front of white people. Rose had been picking through hers, looking for seeds. They shouldn't give seeds to the old. Rose's hair, what was left of it, stuck out in tufts from the top of her head. She'd yet to say a word about the Baldwin book.

Eve poked her fork into a melon chunk. "I got a letter from my sister, the one who lives in Paris. Why not live in Paris if you can? That's what she wondered, so she moved there." She held out a bite to Pauline. Pauline waved the offer away. "You've lived here all your life," Eve said. "Why? It's so backward. About people and so forth." At meals, Eve had a way of letting everyone know that she'd led a bigger life—her book about Chile, for instance. She pronounced it *Cheeleh*, the way it was in Spanish. No one knew what she was saying at first, a book about *Cheeleh*.

Rose stirred her iced tea noisily. "The Bible says—"

"I had my shop," Pauline said. "Just off a two-lane, north of town." Rose was going to say God leads us where we're supposed to be. It was irritating, the way she always harped back to the Bible. It was all chance, anyway, where folks ended up. Pauline's shop had been a chair in the house. You couldn't make a living cutting black hair in Kiser. There weren't enough that could pay for it. She had done some cleaning and sewing on the side.

"Didn't you ever want to live somewhere else?" Eve asked. "Somewhere you'd be treated better?"

And where would that be, Pauline thought, Virginia? "You mean move to Paris like some kind of writer or something?" She looked to see if Rose had caught the allusion to Mr. Baldwin. "My family's all here. My husband's too, buried on a little speck of land they own. I'll be there too, one day."

Rose had her head up, that skinny chin stuck out. "I think—"

"The graveyard's swept clean," Pauline said. "You can see footprints in the dust, when folks come calling." Rose went back to her watermelon, piling the seeds into a hill at the edge of her plate.

"There's no grass growing on the graves," Pauline said. She bet they didn't have one of those in Richmond. Near Kiser there were two, one for black, one for white.

They were in the TV room, watching Oprah, when Lila reached into her big denim bag, studs all over it to scratch things, and held out a box wrapped in pink paper and tied with a yellow bow. "For you, Eve honey." They watched as Eve tore at the tape with a flourish.

"You said you play every week at home," Lila said. "You can teach us."

The Mah Jongg set was an inexpensive one, plastic tiles glued onto wood. There was an elegant line of red script across the box: Game of a Thousand Wonders.

"How sweet of you," Eve said. "Though it's a complicated game."

"We just need a little help," Woodrow said. He winked at Eve. His left eye, the expressive one, had a prominent liver spot in the corner. "We'll be fine."

"Of course," Eve said. She gave him a girly smile. Her eyebrows, which had been lifted by surgery, didn't move much, but she had a way of giving Woodrow a sidelong glance. Sometimes she would open her eyes wide at him, as though he had just said something that pleased her to the core. It had put an extra spring in Woodrow's shuffle.

"And Rose can help me teach you," Eve said.

"Been a long time," Rose said.

Pauline was startled. Just when had Rose learned a game like Mah Jongg? And how was it Eve knew? The two of them must have been talking. Just like Rose to swallow all that sister stuff. "Give me the instructions," Pauline said. "Over the weekend, I'll figure it out."

They passed the game around. Woodrow held up a tile. In the corner was a number, nine.

"It's Nine Wan," Eve said. "Nine characters. See the writing?" She began a long-winded explanation about building the wall and the significance of different winds.

When Eve finally ran out of steam, Lila reached into her big bag again and took out two sweaters. She held one up—olive green, much too petite for her to ever have worn.

"These were my sister's," she said. She handed them to Rose. "I thought you might could use them." Last month there had been two blouses, one with palm trees on it. Pauline had scolded Rose for taking them. "You don't need that woman's hand-me-downs." Rose had shrugged. "It's no use to fight when white folks want to do," she said. Oh Lord, Pauline thought. You sent me a *gitalong*. Her mother used to tell her, don't be one of those *gitalongs*. Her mother would not bring home leftovers from the white families she worked for no matter how delicious they might be. "Maybe just once in a while," Pauline's father would say. "Some of that brisket you fix for them? For your babies here?" No, her mother snapped. Not even when they offer.

Now Rose was saying thank you. Not just thank you but *I surely do thank you*. Pauline had to look away.

Later, she followed Rose to her room. Rose put the olive green sweater up to her chest and measured the sleeves against her arms. There was no point to scolding her again. The olive sweater would be big on her, but she would wear it and Lila would be pleased with herself. Rose was just the kind of black woman these people liked.

"When you ever learn that Mah Jongg?" Pauline asked.

"One of those kids of the lady I worked for, the sickly one, he love to play a game." She fingered the cable stitching that ran down the front of the sweater. "Was a time he didn't want a thing but Mah Jongg. Mrs. Wright, she'd have me play with them, on account of that game's no good for two. This one might be *too* warm."

"Missy Eve likes it, means we're going to play," Pauline said. "Have to please the queen."

Rose held up the bright pink pullover. "We got more than one in this hive." She spread the sweater on her bed. It was a color Pauline never would have worn.

"You ought to give that sweater back."

"She give it to me. Might hurt her feelings if I give it back."

Pauline pointed her wheelchair toward the door. Lila would feel good, and Eve would go home bragging about her new black friend. "Guess you going to take whatever they give you," she said, and rolled out.

By Monday, Pauline had learned the basics of Mah Jongg. There was a lot of silly fuss about prevailing winds and breaking the wall. Pauline saw ways the game could be simplified and meant to suggest a thing or two.

Only four could play. Pauline made sure to sit down with Eve and Woodrow at the card table before Rose could get there.

"There's five of us," Eve said, "when Lila gets here."

"Rose can take my place, after a while," Pauline said. Rose set her walker by the door and sat beside it in a straight chair. She looked a little hurt, but said nothing. It was so easy with her, Pauline almost felt guilty. When Lila frisked in, Eve started another animated lecture. "The North and South Winds shuffle the tiles. It's called the Twittering of the Sparrows." She flitted her fingers like birds and gave Woodrow one of her sidelong glances.

"Very clever, these Chinese," Woodrow said.

"Well, no, Woodrow." Eve dropped her hands. "That

is a stereotype. In Beijing I found just as many dull-witted people as anywhere in the United States." The trip to China was one they hadn't heard about. Maybe the only one.

"All those places you've been," Woodrow said. He picked up one of the tiles and examined it. It was the blank one, White Dragon. "So many strangers," he said. "I guess I like it just fine here in the good old USA."

"You might be xenophobic," Eve said. "Now, everyone throws the dice to see who'll be East Wind, to see who'll go first."

Woodrow set White Dragon back on the table. The big word had whooshed right over him.

"How do you spell that?" Lila asked. "That kind of phobic."

"With an X," Rose said from her spot along the wall. "You spell it with an X."

They were slow to learn the rules. Eve was a hawk, reminding them of the names of the tiles, the anti-clockwise order of winds. Woodrow was flummoxed. "Perhaps," he said, "I need a private lesson." He looked expectantly at Eve. She reached over and patted his hand. "Keep at it."

They played three times a week. The scorching days of September gave way to a muggy fall. A physical therapist drove over from Nacogdoches three days each week to work with Eve. The price of that Pauline could not imagine, but in October, Eve announced that her doctor had looked at her X-rays and pronounced her sound enough for travel. Her daughter, Mimi, was flying down the next day to pick her up and they would fly back to Richmond together. "I'll stay with Mimi for a while," Eve said. "It'll be better." Lenny was not yet free from Her Majesty, the Mama. "We've never been apart this long," she added. "It's been hard, of course."

"For your last day," Lila said, "for tomorrow, let's have one more game."

"One more," Eve said. "Then you'll be equipped to carry on without me."

The next afternoon, when Pauline rolled into the game room, Eve was wiping down a table. "This place is so filthy. I wish Mimi didn't have to see it." Woodrow was sitting in the corner, watching her. He'd been down in the mouth all day.

Lila dropped her wet umbrella in the corner. "Should we light candles or something? Today's the first day of Sukkot. It's on this calendar I have. Eve, honey, what are you doing with that tissue?"

"They just laid off another housekeeper," Woodrow said.

"We can skip the candles," Eve said. "A happy holiday. No tragedies." She saw Woodrow's puzzled face. "A harvest holiday. A sukkah is a temporary shelter Jews sometimes put up in their back yards to celebrate. In ancient times the farmers built them so they wouldn't have to leave the fields."

"Sukkot. That's the plural," Lila said. She loved her library's Internet. She would collect little facts and present them to the group, like a cat with a prize mouse.

Rose had come in, wearing the palm tree blouse. The polyester collar was full of pills. She had rarely appeared for Mah Jongg after the first week.

"The shelters are supposed to be porous," Lila said. "so you can see the stars. It's in the Old Testament. In Numbers."

"Leviticus," Rose said. "It's in Leviticus."

"It's that part where God talks about his people in the desert," Eve said. "Numbers? I don't know. They called them booths."

"That's not Numbers. It's Leviticus." Rose had got out her bible, which she carried in a pocket on the side of her walker. On the cover of the book, in gold lettering, was her maiden name: Rose Louise Sparks. Pauline figured she was related to Woodrow, way back there somewhere. Rose didn't want to know.

One of the new aides, the one with the blond streak in her black hair, burst into the room holding the cordless phone. "Long distance," she said and handed it to Eve. Eve was used to her cell phone; Kiser didn't have service yet. Pauline had seen Eve wipe off a receiver before she picked up a phone the others might have used. She couldn't do that now, not with Miss Streaky standing over her.

"Here," Rose said. "Leviticus 24. *That I made the people of Israel dwell in booths when I brought them out of the land of Egypt.*"

Eve turned away from the table and scrunched her shoulder against the phone. "If you want to," Pauline heard her say. "Okay."

Out the window, the rain was coming down in sheets. Pauline tried to get her worn-out ears to pick up the sound of splashing, to hear the rain rolling over the gutters, falling between the miserly plantings of juniper along the foundation. She thought she heard thunder. Here was lightning. One thousand one, one thousand two. Nothing. Did the thunder come or not?

Rose kept her nose stuck in the Bible. Never a moment wasted when the Old Testament was at hand.

"You ever read that James Baldwin book I give you?" Pauline asked. She had been picking at a frayed spot on the card table, rubbing a loose piece of the vinyl cover between her fingers. There had been another table once, another thunderstorm, a different foursome, the power going out in the middle of a game. Sheila, Trudy, Lavette. Girlfriends, all gone now.

"Started it," Rose said. "Didn't get far."

The friends had played gin rummy in the storm, and finished by candlelight, laughing. They were women of passion and they had that in common.

"You ought to read it through," Pauline said to Rose. "Might be something there for you."

Eve put down the phone, her expression dark. Her altered brows never really frowned, but her mouth, untouched by the knife, would fall at the corners, a droop of deep lines around it. She seemed reduced, as if the cordless had pulled the spunk from her. The shoulders she would lift when she lectured them were drawing in, sinking.

"That was Mimi," Eve said. "Lenny's mother is better. He's flying down here instead of her."

Eve's left hand, the one with the big ring, was a ball in her lap. Woodrow had been watching her, working his lips over the teeth he was proud to still have. "So we get to meet your Lenny," he said.

"We'll have to get going right away," Eve said.

"We want to meet him," Lila said. "When's he get here?"

"Seven. Seven o'clock tonight." Eve was looking at her tiles. She seemed lost in thought.

"I don't know," Woodrow said. "Maybe he won't live up to his billing." He tried to catch Eve's eye. She wouldn't look up. "So whose turn is it? Isn't Eve North Wind this time?"

"That's me," Lila said. "Don't you want us to meet him?" She discarded the tile with six dots. Woodrow picked it up and called Pung.

Pauline pointed with her scoring pencil. "That's a Chow. You don't get as many points."

"Oh, right," he said. He tried to catch Eve's eye. "Eve, you didn't correct me." She hadn't moved. When she finally picked up a tile, her hand was shaking. She held her draw absently for a moment, then discarded it. There was moisture on it from her sweaty fingers.

"So what will you do tonight?" Lila asked. "You can't fly right back east. Will you spend the night in Shreveport?"

"At one of those casino hotels," Woodrow said. "One of those big ones on the river?"

Eve was reaching for the red leather bag she carried around. "I don't know. Some place big, some place no one will really notice us." She spoke so quietly Pauline almost couldn't hear her. It was an odd thing for Eve to say. Pauline watched her fish out a bottle of Tylenol.

"Your hip hurting?" Lila asked.

"It just started up again. Could you be a dear and get me a glass of water?"

"Your hip don't want to go," Woodrow said. "Your hip wants to stay here with us." He gave her one of his winks, but there was no sidelong glance to answer. Eve fussed with the cap of the pill bottle, as if it were a task that needed all her focus. Something wasn't right, Pauline thought. She had seen swollen eyes and split lips, marriages that didn't end when they should have. She'd seen women who were scared to go home. Her sister had been married to a bully.

"I bet when you fell on the stairs, people made a big fuss," Pauline said. "Folks always have a lot of advice, a time like that."

Lila came back with the water. She set it down and put her hand on Eve's shoulder. "I know. They all stand around over you. People want to help, and you're so embarrassed."

"It was just Lenny and me. There wasn't anyone else around." Eve put her palm up to her mouth and dumped in the Tylenol. Normally she centered a pill delicately on her tongue, as if it were a bon-bon. Perhaps she'd taken an extra, and didn't want them to see.

"Just the two of you?" Rose said. She had moved to a chair that was closer, where she could watch the game over Woodrow's shoulder.

"It was raining," Lila said. "Isn't that what you told us?"

"We were going to the car. I slipped. That's what happened. I slipped on those stairs. Lucky I didn't crack my head."

"Good thing," Lila said. "You're so smart and you know so much." She had settled back into her chair and was studying Eve. "You've got a good husband, right? Maybe Lenny's okay with all that. Sometimes a man gets tired of it."

"Sometimes a man think he got to equal things out a little," Rose said. Lila gave Rose a look. Pauline knew they had figured something out.

Eve's hands were on the table, clasped to each other. "He's not like that." For a few seconds, no one spoke. Eve gazed down at the broken Chinese wall. "He's a decent man, Lenny is." Pauline had never heard her speak so softly, a throat squeezed nearly shut.

"Whose turn?" Woodrow said.

"Mine," Pauline said, and discarded something, not paying attention to what.

"Woo-hoo!" Woodrow picked up the tile and called Mah Jongg, or *Mah-Gong* as he liked to say.

"Eve, honey," Lila said. "Your hands are shaking. What is it? You can tell us."

Eve put her hands over her face. There was a howl,

from deep in her chest. When Pauline touched her elbow, Eve turned away. Of course, Pauline thought. Not now. Not for all the liberal causes on earth. She saw that Rose was watching. "I suppose *you* think it's God's will," she said.

Eve turned to Lila, who took her in her arms.

They had four hours before Lenny arrived, but it was not enough to change Eve's mind. Lila begged her to come home with her, to take time to think. Eve would not even consider it. "And I don't want you to see me off," she said. "Let's just have dinner together before I leave."

Lila stayed for dinner, and they all tried to match her determined cheer, but it was an awkward meal. Woodrow, who had finally caught on after Eve began to weep, now sat in silence, unable to pretend, even for a moment, that everything would be all right.

After dinner, after they said their goodbyes, Lila went home and Woodrow went to his room. They were peacemakers, those two, Pauline thought. They have had it all their lives, the comfort of their status quo. Pauline had had it too, their status quo. She parked her wheelchair near the lobby, in the hallway where Eve would not see her.

He was not a big man, just a little taller than Eve, but a handsome man, white hair swept back in waves from a tanned, agreeable face. Pauline wondered if Eve could have been wrong, if she could have imagined something that wasn't there. He kissed his wife, adjusted her collar that was turned up in back. She had been alone and unhappy when they met. He had called her his princess.

Pauline's wheelchair made a little whine when it got going, and they looked up when she rolled into the lobby. Lenny was helping Eve with her raincoat, his arm moving around her as she started along. She's never done anything to hurt me, Pauline thought. Her airs and her academia, her Cheeleh, her White Dragons and twittering birds, she had never done a thing except assume more than she was entitled to.

Pauline scooted her machine over until they couldn't help but speak to her. The introductions were brief and cool. She looked right into Lenny's jay-blue eyes, the ones she'd heard so much about. He tried a charming smile on her, but she didn't smile back. "I feel like I know you," Pauline said. "She's talked so much about you." Lenny shifted his gaze, but Pauline didn't. "So very, very much."

"Eve likes to talk," he said, and smoothed his trench coat down the front, like he was wiping off a spill.

Pauline searched for something in his face that she might recognize as shame, apology or remorse, but saw nothing. "I feel like I know everything," she said. Those were the words that got to him. Oh, he tried to cover it, but she could tell.

"I'm sorry?" he said. "You know I don't hear so well." He fiddled with a coat button, then brushed at something on his sleeve. She just couldn't let him go. For her son and Truman Wally, even for Rose, she just could not let him.

Eve did not even give Pauline a warning look, she was that wrung out.

After they left, Pauline rolled down the hall toward Woodrow's room. Rose was there, knocking lightly on his door. He didn't answer.

Pauline motioned for Rose to crack the door. "Woodrow?"

They found him sitting by his window, which looked out on the front parking lot. Pauline had never been in Woodrow's room. It was neat, which she would not have expected. On the bureau was a portrait of his wife, dead six years. At the window, Woodrow had a hand on the sill, as if he'd been tempted to raise the sash. "Could she have exaggerated what he did?" he said. "Could she have done that?"

"Anything's possible," Pauline said.

Woodrow turned from the window. He wiped a handkerchief across his nose, over the oxygen line. The liver-colored spot at the corner of his eye was moist. "You'll keep the game going and all, won't you?"

Pauline had pulled close to Rose; the three of them and their equipment could barely fit in the tiny room. She noticed fuzz growing on a bald spot by Rose's ear. Her hair had started to come back, but she hadn't mentioned it.

"I don't believe so," Pauline said. "I don't believe we will."


When the others found out what Pauline had said to Lenny, they chastised her, telling her she'd made things worse for Eve. Pauline never meant Eve any harm, but she was angry with her. It is hard enough to make your way in this world, butting up against what is beyond is your control. A woman like Eve did not need to be married to such a man. It reminded Pauline of her friend, Sheila, when she was dying of one of God's nastier diseases. When Sheila heard that her nephew—young, fit, his life ahead of him—had committed suicide, she guffawed before she wept. Vigor is wasted on the healthy; freedom is wasted on the free.

In the two years since Eve left Chadwick, Woodrow has found a sweetheart, which Pauline thinks is a godsend, because his health is failing even more, and his grandson will soon head out for Iraq. Lila's older son, Grady, quit the Kiwanis in a public huff after trying to budge their racist attitudes. Recently Lila has asked Pauline what kind of life she had, growing up in the part of town she did. Rose died a year after Eve left, and Pauline misses her.

Chadwick has struggled on, but the family pulled its money out, so the Manor is on a downward slide. Pauline believes Eve sent a hefty donation; she wishes Eve would send more. She keeps her on her praying list. Eve stayed with Lenny, as far as anyone knows. Lila gets a Hanukkah card from her each year, an affectionate joke between them. Eve thought of them when the Columbia broke apart, dropping its debris. She sent a postcard, an art card with a painting by Frida Kahlo on it. "Saw you're in the news," she wrote. "Who would have guessed?"

# A DOWNWARD PATH

I t's not true there were no casualties on the ground when the space shuttle fell apart over Texas. Some things happened that morning, some happened later. If you connect the dots, for us here in Kiser, more trouble came of that day than most folks know. This is what you might think if you didn't live here: The government hurried here to help us, took over the burden, started the search, brought in food and organized things.

That's not how it went.

At first, nobody believed what fell on us intact—cabinets, computers, toilets—things we could look at and say, we know what that is. Our police chief called up NASA and said, We have your people here.

Unlikely, NASA said. Would have burned up.

Ah, beg to differ, Chief Orbaugh said—or less polite words to that effect. He explained, in the growl he used when the town council annoyed him: A man found a leg out on 621 and what do you want him to do, put it in his 4x4 and bring it to you? Cars have run over, not knowing.

My brother, Spencer Scott, was the district's chief forest ranger. Two NASA types sped up here from Houston, and he escorted them to the highway, where someone had thrown a blanket over the leg and a sheriff's deputy was diverting traffic around it. The men looked at each other. "Oh Christ," one said. They got out their cell phones, which were never going to work out on 621, not back then.

"Supposed to rain tonight," Spencer said. "The land is prone to flood."

Orders were given and searching began. The feds were stretched thin. Since the U.S. government employed him, Spencer was put in charge of the media who came to Chireno County. Really, he said to his bosses, I have no idea. Every day he thought someone from Washington would come in and take over. Instead they gave him rules to tame the merciless pack. No talk about bodies. No buzzards in the sky, no maggots on the ground. No burned hands or charred remains. In fact, there are no remains. You will call them items of interest.

They meant what they said. When a young reporter for a local paper put vultures in her dispatch, phone calls were made from on high. We never saw her byline again.

Spencer was struggling. "Teresa," he said to me. "I'm over my head." My brother's not as tough as me, not at all a conniver. I married a Sparks, a low-lying, slithery type, and I am acquainted with deception. When Spencer asked me to drive up to Eno and borrow that hearse that Russ Cauthen keeps in his garage just for kicks, I knew he had turned a corner. I delivered it to Norris Tibbet, who drove it down a logging road and told the reporters they couldn't follow. They waited for him to come out of the woods and when he did, they trailed him like Plott hounds to Tibbett's funeral home, pestering to know what was in the body bag. Norris told them, in bits and sass, about how deep in the woods he'd gone this time and you know by now ladies and gentlemen that I can't tell you what we found or what kind of shape he or she was in, but it's an honor to serve my country. Norris stood there in his briar-shredded suit spinning yarns till dark. The body parts traveled in peace to Spring Creek Baptist, at the end of a dirt-and-gravel road. The government sent a refrigeration truck, and the church became a makeshift morgue. The funeral of Mary Lynn Davis was postponed.

Spencer faced the reporters with what he could manage. A fine-tooth search of rural America was producing the usual—abandoned houses with meth labs inside, and in the woods, bones of the disappeared. "Long-ago murdered or wandered off, we don't know," Spencer told the pack of hounds. "No drugs I'm aware of." Rumors were rampant, some of them true. Three scientists in white coats came over a rise and scared a small herd of cattle into a stampede. One long-horn veered off and went after the whitecoats, who barely made it to the fence. Our cattle fared better than our goats, who will eat anything, no matter the chemicals. A few of them died. "A funny story," Spencer said, just as he was told. "Sounds good, don't believe it."

Spencer had a headache that wouldn't go away and a pain in his chest, like someone standing on it. "When's it going to end?" he asked me one night, six days into the mess. The reporters stuck a microphone in front of anyone who would jabber. Our county judge went on TV and preened around like the banty-rooster idiot he is. The media had a field day, since their group harbored eager mimics.

"Our people aren't equipped for this kind of scrutiny," Spencer said to me, his voice just a croak by then. Next day Chief Orbaugh stood on the courthouse steps and ordered the media to leave.

"Who told you do to that?" Spencer tried to yell. Orbaugh roared back, about trouble and rumors and noses where they didn't belong. In Eno, the Chamber of Commerce brewed coffee for the prying eyes and answered all their questions. There were brochures about nearby attractions and kindly old ladies with rooms for the night. Eno has a new rec center now, and we have a broken-down park.

The reporters caught wind that a one-car wreck had been discovered near Kiser, just after debris began to fall. They were calling from Eno by then. "The wreck is not related," Spencer said. "I give you my word." The elephant on his chest pressed down.

At my house, a band of searchers from Arizona found

a glove in a field behind us, and yes there was something inside it. Spencer was the one who told Newland and me that we had to leave, while the FBI scoured our roof and took downspouts off the gutters. They wanted every little thing, though we don't know what they found. All the ruins went back to Florida, where the engineers laid them out in a hangar and worked backwards as best they could. "The debris won't lie," Spencer said. This piece fell in Lufkin, that one in Yellowpine, here are the tiles that floated down in Kiser. What gruesome facts they figured out, with their maps and calculations and eighty-four thousand pieces. The crew capsule tore apart in twenty-four seconds, as it dropped ten thousand meters. Pray the astronauts were dead by then, oxygen gone, brains not knowing. There was a recording of voices just at the end. Someone had to listen.

If this, then that. Life and death a line of dominoes. Mary Lynn's funeral was put off for a week, so she could be buried at Spring Creek Baptist when the FEMA truck was gone. Her brother went up a ladder on the day he should have been in his good gray suit walking a casket down the aisle. His head isn't right since the fall.

If this, then that.

It's been three years since the shuttle fell. I filed for divorce, a surprise to no one, and Spencer just retired. He is only fifty-five. People think it was the accident last summer, when a three-hundred-pound wild boar totaled his car. Fifty miles an hour his car was going, out on 621, and the thing came straight at him. He had two broken ribs, a sprain in his back, two pins in his ankle. But he was already fried, my brother. Something else had come at him, out of the blue. Not one hog, but a sounder.

# IN PARKER'S WOOD

P ine warbler opens song, the first to speak, a one-note trill that goads aside the shroud of dawn. She perches on a tulip tree that's uncommon in this forest, its life a chance of brawny wind from far-off meadow, Sputnik in the sky that year. At the tip of crown, a tiny bulge of someday leaf protrudes toward winter's day, though limbs still hold dried cups of spent samaras— dead flowers pointing skyward, spoils of hope. Where warbler sings, a branch is broken, and down below, another: jagged rips made yesterday, that came with shake and roar. Sweet gum brushes where these branches grew and in the slightest stir of air a gum ball drops, stiff sphere of autumn's brown. Drunk with pleasure at morning mist, roots register all landings—this weight tiny, that one big . Vibration forms their language.

What mortal hears the swell of water rising root to crown? The suck of cambria? The cry of bark and broken limbs?

The boy would hear.

Warbler flits, another spot, above a mound of man that's clothed in flight-suit orange. Shorn arms, severed leg, a bright-colored freak from the sky: torso in a crook, husk of hope and dreams. A shoulder covers the hole where nuthatch raised her brood last year. Treehopper's eggs frost a twig with white; a leg is dangling close. Curve of helmet catches light, dew a blanket on it. Rising sun makes one drop fall. Plop on the hide of armadillo scouting lace bugs in the leaves. He noses toward a tear of cloth, a fleck of blood found, too.

Crow loves a shiny thing; the helmet draws her eye. She braves a walk on orange mound, tail feathers swinging slow and bluesy. Percussion next: she taps the sphere; woodpecker stops and listens. Crow hops atop the tinted orb—man's face behind a darkened shield—but she slips and lands on orange heap. It makes a better playground. She jabs at something high on a sleeve—red stripe, a bit of star, all that's left and nothing shines, though something smells of scorch and metal. A plastic tube runs down this side; it's smooth inside her beak. She plucks and drops, grabs again, casts it to the mound. There's zipper here and she tugs at that and crosses mound again. Under orange is a curious mix that pokes from elbow's remnant: muscle, artery and bone. She snatches out a blue-black thread, waves her toy, forsakes it for another, opens her beak and lets that one fall. Breakfast is in the flesh just here; she leaves her squirt and consumes her fill.

Who would hear the peck on a helmet, the clutch of thread, the cone of samara as it falls to the chest of a bright-colored freak in the tree? The boy would hear. He comes on pony now, looking down.

Then up.

# THE MIDDLE OF THAT MESS

When Rose Sparks Benjamin looked at Woodrow D. Sparks, she saw an old white man who'd been spared a lot of trouble in his life. He had never been hungry, he'd never been out of work. All his life he could go anywhere he wanted, eat anywhere he pleased, live wherever he could afford. None of the elders in her family had lived like that.

She had never spoken to him about the name they shared.

This particular morning, Woodrow's eyes drifted around the Chadwick Manor sitting room in search of an audience, and found only Rose. She felt sorry for him. There had been that business with Eve—he had an eye for the ladies—and then his grandson with the drugs, and now this awful thing last Saturday about his niece. He just couldn't get past it; he was about to tell the child's story for the umpteenth time. Here in this nursing home, only so many could hear him.

He always began with the flowers, and what a reliable girl Maddie was. "The flowers hadn't got to the church, and the wedding was at eleven thirty. Maddie was to bring them by nine thirty. None of us could believe she wasn't there."

The wedding was a bit of a rush job, the bride already three months along. This fact would be at the end of Woodrow's story, though Rose wondered why he ever mentioned it at all. She'll wish, he would say, that she'd picked another day to be married. For the rest of her life, she'll wish that. She could have waited those two more weeks until Valentine's Day, even if she was afraid she'd start to show.

"People drove in sad. They were talking about what they'd seen on the way in. What they saw on TV. What they saw along the roads." The space shuttle had blown apart, just that morning, and a few bits of it lay around the church. When the guests arrived they burst to tell.

"How's a bride supposed to have her happiest day in the middle of all that mess?" Woodrow picked up a stack of wedding photographs his daughter had brought him and handed them to Rose. It was a new part of his story.

"The bride's mighty pretty," Rose said, studying them. The white folks were not as dressed up as they might be, for going to church. A few of the older ladies were wearing pants. Perhaps it was all they had.

"They couldn't afford many flowers, but the bride, her name's Brenda, she's Maddie's friend, she wanted those white roses. Maddie got them at cost, since she worked for the florist in Eno. She was going to put them up in the church and she'd fixed Brenda a nice bouquet.

"Roses are nice. Pretty with baby's breath."

"They didn't tell Brenda. They didn't tell Brenda about Maddie. They just told her there'd been a mix-up with the florist. Brenda walked down the aisle with a magnolia branch in her hand, magnolia and some pink flowers my daughter ran over to the neighbors' and picked."

"Looks like camellia. Blooms about this time."

"It give her something to hang onto. Nobody could tell what was missing."

This was the part where Woodrow would talk about Maddie's accident. He would be almost teary, and might reach for his oxygen. Rose would let him go on and tell it—what the burning car looked like crushed against the road sign, how a boy driving to market had pulled her out, how someone else drove to the nearest house to call. While he stammered on, Rose thought of another wedding, this one long ago but also in February, on Valentine's Day. It was back in the thirties. Her mother's cousin, William, was set to marry in a little church on the road to Yellowpine. Only he didn't show, and no one ever heard from him again. Not his mama, not his sweetheart, not his brothers and sisters. He just vanished.

"And the car," Rose said. "Where was it they found it?" Woodrow had started to falter; she thought it best to encourage him toward the end.

"Way out Prospect Road. It's kind of a short cut to Eno from her house. But ain't no houses on that stretch where they found her. There she is, driving alone on the road, space shuttle comes apart and ten minutes later somebody finds her car, run off the road and on fire."

"Such a young girl," Rose said. "Eighteen you said?" He would go on now and talk about the family, what good people they were. It was his wife's side of the family, and they had been kind to him since she died.

Rose had been just a girl, maybe eight years old, when William did not show up to marry his sweetheart. Rose's mother had made her a dress, blue it was, and it was to be her Easter dress that year, too. She remembered how at the church they sat and sat, people whispering, though she did not know at the time, all that they were saying.

What they were saying was, there's another one, disappeared. How many more of our men will just vanish? William had a job at a logging outfit. There was a rumor that a white man wanted that job.

"The boy got her out of the car. Reached into that burning car and pulled her out. She was unconscious. She didn't have a chance.

"I want to know. I want to know did something hit her? They kept saying on TV, a wonder nobody on the ground was hurt. But maybe that's not true. First there was that awful noise. Was she scared by the noise? Then maybe something came at her. Might be she's so scared she runs off the road.

"It didn't all just float down. There had to be hot metal.

Into her windshield, into her eyes? Or maybe her engine. Slice right in. Grover Sharkey, used to be my neighbor, he was on TV. Said something whizzed past him like a bullet. And him an Army veteran, he knew. Now the government's setting up all over this county, searching for the pieces of their precious space ship. And they ain't saying a word to us."

Rose said, "Nobody will do anything for you, will they?"

"Won't nobody tell us a thing. Rescue squad, police, the hospital, they all just shut right up. That boy that found her, he wants to know, too. He stayed with her while his daddy drove to a phone. My daughter, she tells me the rescue squad came, and they wondered, too, but now they won't say a word."

"They been shut up."

"They *all* been shut up."

Poor Woodrow, Rose thought. Something has altered his world. He thinks differently now, of the people in charge.

When Rose's aunt and uncle told the police their son was missing, the officer had smirked. Just flew the coop, did he? No, her aunt said, not likely. Well, the officer said, maybe he had another girlfriend. Sounds like he didn't want to get married. Then the policeman with the great imagination offered up another theory: Your boy could have taken off for greener pastures. There are jobs up north, you know. Recruiters been down, looking for strong, young bodies.

No, her aunt said. He would not.

Nothing was ever done about William, not an official finger lifted. The women in Rose's family would count on their own calloused fingers the men who had disappeared: Jacob Washington, and Esther Tinsley's youngest boy, and Letha Roberts's second cousin whose name they could not recall, but he was one, too. Went to work one night and never came back. Six in all, in seven years. That was just the ones they knew.

Rose's bible was on her lap. She had come into this room for her usual prayers, which she said this time of day in a high-backed, blue chair she liked. The bible had her name on it. Sparks, her maiden name, was there in gold letters.

Woodrow was looking her way, like he was taking in something for the first time. His eyes were still moist, and he was working his jaw, back and forth.

His face had softened, as if some great need had been satisfied with the telling, once more, of his story. He removed the oxygen line from his nose. Smoking had got to his heart and he was tethered to his tank. "Do you ever," he said. "Do you ever think about how things were, way back there?" He was looking at her bible now.

"Back there," Rose said, "it was some bad times." She spread her fingers across the bible's pebbled grain, fingering a cross embossed on the top. Poor fool. "Why don't we pray," she said.

# FROM A DISTANCE

I didn't recognize the handwriting on the pink envelope in the mail today, and this small mystery lifted my spirits. Inside the envelope was a snapshot of a slumbering newborn, her web of forehead veins framed by a crocheted cap. Creases bisected the puffs under her swollen eyes, but her tiny lips were set in a near-smile, as if to say, so far, so good. On the back of the photograph was a note in James Trenholder's cramped hand: *We are in heaven.* His new wife had added a line: *Hope to meet you someday—are you on Facebook?*

I laid the baby's picture where Bobbi would see it when she dragged in from planting the courthouse pansy beds, a fall garden club project she normally relished. Her spirits were sagging, too, after the death of our great niece, Ally, in a swimming accident. Each family death piggy-backs on the ones that came before, and at our age, they were adding up. I hoped Bobbi would find cheer in this baby's arrival. She might say, with her usual pluck, that it signals a healing for James, past the sadness of his divorce from Lauren, whom we remembered so well. James, with his penchant for order, might think of the baby as a marker for life's turn. He is young. Later he likely will learn that significance can be less distinct, or even invisible, until an unfamiliar critter pokes its head into a certain slant of light and a man sees how, on a particular day, the balance of his world was altered.

I poured a glass of water and took it into the garage, where there's an old wicker chair I like to sit in. I thought of our niece, Suzanne, who was having a difficult time with the death of her only child. Bobbi and I didn't arrange our lives with the markers of children, but my wife taught fifth grade so she will tell you, she had oodles of them. For many years she taught in Ohio, where I had a job with General Aluminum. We retired to Kiser, where we both grew up and have family still. Our money goes farther down here and winters are easy, though we miss the bit of culture our town had. We've kept up with our Ohio neighbors, including the Trenholders, through the Christmas notes that Bobbi still sends on UNICEF cards, newsy and unfailingly early. She has a soft spot for James, who was one of her fifth-graders. He was a quiet boy, full of serious intelligence and a dream for something grand. The big dream might have come naturally for him in our midwest town, Wapakoneta, which achieved fame in 1969 and still trades on that moment of glory. Little James could tell you that it was one and two-tenths of a mile from his front porch to the corner bedroom in the clapboard house where young Neil Armstrong hung his model airplanes so they looked like they were flying. The First Man was that boy's hero.

As I look back now on what happened, the troubling day we last saw James, I believe that James longed to serve, to be part of something bigger than himself. He had wanted, of course, to be an astronaut. But James had asthma, so space was not in his future, nor being a soldier either, which he also wanted. He became a chemical engineer and took a job in DeRidder, Louisiana. The work was interesting, but it was not his dream. Perhaps that is why, when the space shuttle tore apart and the call went out for volunteer searchers, James turned to Lauren and said, "I have to go."

He came as soon as they would let him, on a Saturday in late February, three weeks after Columbia fell. The first round of volunteers had worn out, or needed to return to their jobs, or, in the case of the National Guard, left to prepare for that unfortunate business in Iraq. On his first search, James found nothing. It was a raw, windy day of Texas snow that would have chilled his face and melted before it hit the ground. The next Saturday he came back, but finished with only sniffles and a deep scratch across his cheek. The searching was tough. Deep East Texas is not much akin to the fabled parts west of here. We have swamps, not sagebrush, and briars as high as your head. We have tall trees, thick underbrush and not much development. When the bureaucrats in Washington wanted to know why the search in Chireno County only covered one square mile in a day, our guys pointed to a pictorial map of our state and said, They don't call it the Pine Thicket for nothing. I'd been out on the first day of searching, and woke up the next day with an ache in every bone. I was just sixty-five, not so old, but after that I left searching to the younger and more resilient. I fulfilled my duty instead at the VFW, which became a command center for the volunteers.

In the mornings, while the searchers gulped coffee and donuts courtesy of the Ladies' Auxiliary, I wound between them collecting dirty napkins and used paper plates. They were here to pick up debris, but they left a lot behind. The VFW was just a pre-fab building that one of our land barons gave in his father's memory. It was never meant for that much traffic—the Texas Baptist Men, Kiwanis from Oklahoma and firefighters from at least six states. They came from everywhere to feel the pulse of our tragedy. The toilets clogged, the woodwork was gouged, the paper towel dispensers broke and fell from the walls. It's been four years, though, and you'd never know that hurricane hit us. NASA fixed it all.

On the fifth Saturday of this drawn-out affair, I saw a familiar face across the room. I hadn't seen James since he was seventeen, though he lived less than two hours away. We looked at each other, this grown boy and I, and recognition broke out. His straight hair is dark brown, like his mother's was, and he has a long neck and a prominent chin, also like his mother. Rosalind was beautiful. My own Bobbi, whom I dearly love, never moved with such lightness. Now Rosalind's boy was walking towards me with his chest thrust out like the Army cadet he'd wanted to be. He had a camera around his neck and a machete by his side.

"Mr. Sharkey. I wondered if I'd see you." When he put out his hand I took it, but because I was trying to be a modern man, and I thought of him like a son, I put my other arm around his shoulder in a half embrace.

"Call me Grover, now," I said. "Man to man."

We caught up on the particulars. After Rosalind died— suddenly, of an aneurysm—Bobbi had added James and Lauren to her Christmas list. He knew we'd built a home down here, I knew they'd bought a house in Louisiana. His father, he said, had a steady girlfriend in Ohio now, and seemed content. I told him about the sound of metal whizzing past me, after the shuttle fell.

"It's ironic," I said. "You wanting to be in space as a kid, and here we are."

"More irony than that. The Houston Space Center is eighty miles from my house. I've been there many times. This place, it's eighty miles from our house, too. What are the chances of that in my life?"

"A triangle of meaning," I said.

"And there's this." James pointed to the side of the machete, where the trademark said *Columbia*. He saw significance everywhere, this boy.

James told me about his work, Lauren's promotion at the bank, and his new role leading a church youth group. He had the mindset of a patriot, a straight-laced kid who would have made a good soldier, or even, from the way he talked, a minister. He would have fit in with certain crowds. The astronauts, I'd read, were inclined to be church-going, spiritual people. Whatever they believed when they went up, they believed more of it when they came down. Neil Armstrong, whose mother was a fervent Christian, was not an outwardly religious man before or after space. "I can forgive him for that," James had said to me once, "though myself, I pray every day." He was thirteen at the time, and he'd just read a book about his hero. Armstrong, it was said, could never quite grasp that the world would forever gush over a man who walked on the moon, and he didn't want any part of it. When James learned that the First Man didn't find enough time for his children and would rarely sign an autograph for charity or any other reason, James said okay, so the First Man wasn't perfect. "Everything has a darker side, just like the moon." I think that James grew up to be a true believer who thought there was a force bigger than himself guiding his way through this troubled world. If something came his way, it came his way from a great distance, but for a reason. I suspect he rejected, for the most part, the chaos and vagaries of chance.

While we were talking, I spotted Bobbi coming through the door. She'd been outside handing out donuts. I waved and pointed to James, but I doubted she could see who it was. She held up her hand, fingers spread, and mouthed the words, five minutes.

"It's Mrs. Sharkey?" James said. "I want to say hello."

"Looks like she's headed to the ladies'. We can wait for her in the back there, at the NASA table. You've seen it?" Near the back wall were two cafeteria tables pushed together, spread with muddied, charred or even perfectly intact objects, a trophy case for the diligent and lucky. The searchers often crowded around the table, a museum of the found, where each night newly recovered artifacts would be labeled and set out. No touching was allowed, nor the taking of pictures, but hovering was fine. It was an incentive program, I supposed, since so many of the hundreds who hiked the landscape would discover nothing.

James walked eagerly ahead of me. "Last time they had a helmet and some pieces from the tail." With a zealot's eye, he studied the display. It included a silver glove for a left hand, a space food packet of beef burgundy, part of a small vacuum cleaner and three pieces of metal labeled "fuel tank." I'm sure James believed he would find something, and he believed it would be important. There was plenty out there. Every night the searchers traded rumors about things that went up and hadn't been found: Michael Kirkland's lucky bear, biology experiments in test tubes and incubators, an astronaut's wedding ring, a black box stenciled in white, "top secret." Taped to the table was a sign about the jail time due to anyone who pocketed so much as a metal bolt. The words *federal property* were underlined.

We stood by the table, struck by the freakishness of what we saw, drawn to ordinary things that had traveled such a distance. They'd gone beyond gravity's pull and tumbled back in a free-fall we could only imagine. We were, perhaps, the gawking romantics Neil Armstrong had grown weary of. What was the taste of wine sauce in space? What sound did a fuel tank make when it came apart? Here was the glove an astronaut might have taken off and floated in the air beside him.

"That glove, I found it yesterday." The man who spoke from across the table wore a cap that said FDNY. He told us his name was Flynn, and he has been my friend since that time, a good friend. He and a buddy had driven two straight days to get here. "The glove was stuck on a piece of barbed wire," he said. "Out in the middle of nowhere."

Flynn had a Brooklyn accent so pronounced that people looked up when he spoke. To us he sounded like a TV cop show. I thought, here was a hero who didn't have his fill at The Pile. Otherwise, why come all this way? I know now I was wrong about Flynn, but that day I considered withholding the question I assumed he was waiting for. "You were there for 9/11?" I asked.

"Lost three guys from my shift." Flynn said it like he was used to saying it, and didn't mean to dwell on it. He re-adjusted the cap over his black curls and said nothing more about it. Flynn had a handsome Irish face, though his nose was puggish. He was broad-shouldered, and he worked out. The women had already noticed him.

"Tough stuff," James said. His own shoulders had stiffened and he moved the machete to his right hand. The firefighters' work had made them mythic; the air around us had registered a change.

I pointed to a midnight blue mission patch on the table. "Looks like they found this in a creek." Its shape was an outline of the shuttle on its launchpad, nose to the stars. One side of the fabric was crusted with mud. "There'll be more," I said. "Next drought."

We were so engrossed with the objects that we didn't see Lauren when she came in. She appeared quietly, a tall blond with bow lips that broke into a sweet smile. James had thought she was going to be home, cleaning out the attic.

"The attic can wait," Lauren said, and slipped her arm around James's elbow. Under the green parka that hit the middle of her thighs, I suspected she had a good figure. Flynn cast an eye over her and stepped to our side of the table.

James looked distracted, as if he were struggling to set aside what he was feeling.

"It's not okay?" Lauren said.

"Of course it's okay," James said, and put his hand over hers. "I'm glad you're here."

"I needed to bring you this," she said. She reached into her pocket and handed him an inhaler.

"Oh," Flynn said. "Better have that." He introduced himself and she asked, of course, about his FDNY cap. My friend Flynn is a charmer; he doesn't miss many angles. He directed her right away to the glove he'd found.

"They'll be starting soon," James said. He tugged at Lauren's sleeve to get her attention. "You going to head back or hang out in here?"

"I'm going to search," she said.

James didn't argue, but he didn't look pleased. He told me later, at the courthouse, that she never should have come. This outing was supposed to be his way of dealing with things, not hers.

Lauren leaned over the mission patch. "This must be from someone's shirt," she said, and reached to touch it before James caught her arm.

"A souvenir, most likely," Flynn said. "They take up about a hundred of them."

"Not exactly," said James. "They took up five hundred mission patches. Plus eight hundred NASA bookmarks." He waved his hand over the beef burgundy. "And two point eight pounds of food per day for each astronaut."

Flynn smiled, in a pleasant but patronizing way. "Someone's been reading up," he said. Fortunately, Bobbi showed up at that moment and we got busy with hugs and introductions.

"I feel like I know you," Lauren said to her. "All the cards and notes, the wedding present you sent. We've used that bowl so many times."

"Come by the house," Bobbi said. "Let the men search. I'm making biscuits for the volunteers' dinner."

"There's an idea," James said, smiling at last. "But remember, whatever she tells you, I was only in fifth grade."

"Thank you," Lauren said, "but I'm going to search."

Bobbi took Lauren's hands and drew them to her chest. "Are you sure? Will you be warm enough? Here." She took off the blue wool scarf I'd given her years ago and put it around Lauren's neck. "What else? Do you have enough layers?"

"I'm fine, really." Lauren touched the scarf to her cheek. "I don't mind the cold. It's the heat in Louisiana I hate. Don't you miss Ohio?"

"I miss good cheese. I miss rye bread and grocery stores with fresh flowers. Come on, let's get you a cup of coffee before you start." My wife is a nurturer, with an instinct for people's hidden troubles. Lauren would end up, unexpectedly, spending that night at our house. She and Bobbi would talk into the night, after I'd turned in. When I couldn't sleep, I got up, as I often do, and came here into the garage. Bobbi is a good listener. For a while, in summers, she and Rosalind would walk in the evenings, ending up on our screened porch where this old wicker chair of mine once stood. I could see them from my garden, as the fireflies rose from the grass. The seat of this chair is generous; a slender woman can tuck up her ankles in it.

Now Bobbi was steering Lauren toward the coffee tent when the PA system came alive. The search teams were being assembled.

"Ready?" Flynn looked at James, then at Lauren. "Let's get out there." He'd just arrived, and already he was at home in our tragedy.

"Good luck," I called, as the three of them headed toward the door. Only Flynn looked happy. They would be assigned to the same team, hiking through the brush. It wasn't until much later that I learned what happened on that search, and even then I don't think I learned it all.

I've heard pieces from every side, and I've struggled to understand, because that is, I think, how we attend to each other. I know that James was not himself that day. He was a young man who had tried to be a good husband, who had wanted a marriage that was rich and joyful and unencumbered by the lousy deck that fate sometimes hands us. He wanted a life that ducked heartbreak when it could, though sometimes a man can only tell by looking back that a sidestep around one heartache has brought another unexpected sorrow.

I watched James go, this son of graceful Rosalind, with his machete and his camera and his belief in divine significance. Of my two boys, Rosalind had said once, James is more sensitive. We were standing in her flower garden, a grocery bag of my home-grown zucchini at her feet. Across the yard, Rosalind's husband, J.T., was playing catch with the boys, teaching James to throw a fastball. Rosalind had a way of standing, one hip cocked, that was feminine but not affected. In the garden she favored cut-offs and a sun bonnet like the pioneer women wore. It gave her a look of innocence but also wisdom, that brim a frame to the crinkles just coming to her face. We heard J.T.'s voice. "Is that the hardest you can throw?" Rosalind closed her eyes, as if to block a thought. On her upper lip was a bead of sweat I longed to brush away. "His father doesn't see," she said, "how hard he's trying to please." She was forty years old that summer; she had eleven years to live.

"I'll have cantaloupe soon," I said. "In about a week."

\* \* \*

The searchers headed out toward Izzy Blanchard's place, a mile west of the Atoka River. They made a line of twenty, ten feet apart. There were rules to follow: Look up as well as down, don't touch anything you find. No taking pictures of debris. And this: Whatever was in front of you, you had to walk through it. Your neighbor might be waltzing down a logging path, but the tangled brush beneath your feet, that was yours to conquer.

James would have followed the rules to the letter, without complaint. Every Saturday brought a couple of yahoos who hadn't known what they were getting into, who griped and moped and sometimes turned back because they had better things to do on a weekend than rip their way through such a mess, with nothing to show for it in the end. But James had that machete, which he wielded like the soldier he wasn't, and a thicket all his own before him. Briars ripped at his boot laces and stickers covered the legs of his jeans. A devil's walking stick, high as his head, just missed his eye and tore his sleeve, but he gripped that machete harder and moved in rhythm, back and forth, up and down. Lauren was on one side, a trouper who could slip between the trees and woody vines that would have stopped a more strapping physique. Flynn was on the other side of James, moving more quickly, always slightly ahead. James searched his ten feet and a little more. He reached the machete towards Lauren's turf. He poked at something he thought she'd passed up.

She caught him at it. "Hey, I'm searching, okay? I'm on top of it. There's nothing there."

"You're not being careful," he said.

"Get out of my space. Search your own."

When his own space yielded a pile of leaves with something silver showing through, James's heart must have beat a little faster. I wonder if he would have been satisfied with a small, unimportant find, if it would have given him the sense of contribution he so badly needed. I wonder what would have happened if he had found it, there and then. "He feels everything," Rosalind had said once. We were in my garage, where she'd come to return a post-hole digger that J.T. had borrowed. There had been an argument at home, between James and his father. "J.T. will never understand him," she said. "Sometimes I think he doesn't try." The late fall sun, filtered through clouds, filled the open door behind her with a yellow-green glow, spectral and thin, the kind of light that's coming through the window now, in this other garage, as I sit in the old chair that Bobbi didn't want to bring south. That day, in Ohio, the light caught the edges of Rosalind's hair, the slope of one supple shoulder, the curve of a breast when she turned. Even her melancholy had a grace to it, a doe resigned to the approach of winter. I did something then, which I shouldn't have done but I don't regret. I reached for her, to feel the luster there, of something that wasn't mine. Before my fingers could land, and I do not regret this, either, Rosalind moved toward my overalls, hanging on a hook. "J.T. could use some of these," she said, running her hand down the rough fabric. "Maybe for Christmas."

※ ※ ※

Over the years, I have talked with my friend Flynn about the search of the pine thicket beside Izzy Blanchard's far pasture. I believe Flynn is a man who follows instincts, a trait which surely serves a firefighter. He kept an eye on James that day, though he could never explain what, if anything, triggered his concern. When Flynn saw that James had stopped, he called out. "You got something?"

"Maybe."

James had squatted, and I imagine he pushed aside a leaf before he made out the lettering on a piece of metal that had been there for years: Bud Light. He read that out loud, to show the others he could laugh at himself.

The group trudged on, uneventfully. Someone found a piece of glass that maybe was, and maybe wasn't, a piece of the windshield. A slender creek appeared beside them, then bent James's way until it was in front of him. He could have jumped it, but he waded in, careful not to slosh his boots around. Studying the murky water, he saw something black that looked like metal. He took off his glove and put in his hand to feel around the algae slime. It was only a rock.

They passed a pond, where clouds of mist rose in stately shapes beside a cypress tree. Later that year, when dry weather came, the edges of the ponds and lakes would give up hidden treasures, by then more curiosity than triumph. Now, James looked across the pond and took a quick photograph of the misty shapes, with Lauren in front of them. Perhaps at that moment he wished again she hadn't come. Weekends were the worst for them and he knew he shouldn't keep leaving her, but it was easier, really, to be apart. Together was what they had been—excited together, laughing together—the day before Halloween when they had not told a soul, no not a soul, that she was pregnant. Lauren explained it to Bobbi this way: Their bubble of joy had charged the atmosphere around them, and they wanted to be alone in it for a while. When the lab called they were eating dinner, Lauren feeling stronger finally at eleven weeks. She was past thirty, though not by much, so they'd agreed to genetic testing, whatever could be done at that stage. Now the news stunned them: Forty-seven chromosomes, one too many. There was an intruder on number twenty-one.

They had talked before the test about this possibility, remote as it had seemed, and admitted they couldn't know how they'd feel, without even knowing what the problem might be. Now, when Lauren turned to James and said, I can't, he thought she meant that she couldn't end a pregnancy. What she meant was, I can't have this baby.

Perhaps this was another time when James asked, what are the chances of that in my life? We put our faith in data, predicted outcomes—one in a thousand for a woman Lauren's age. Maybe James had looked at other people who threw in the towel and thought, Not me, I would choose the high road, I would deal with the hand that God dealt me. He must have thought Lauren, too, would come down on the side of dealing with it, and perhaps she'd believed she would, and now, here she was, and she could not. And he still loved her, and he looked at her, she who would be more than half as mothers always were, and he couldn't do that to her. He could not insist, he could not even argue. And so he said, Okay.

James had wanted to make her happy, he had wanted to believe that this was the way their life would work out. He loved the dream of their happiness so much that when the doctor asked, Do you want to make an appointment, James said it for her, so she would not have to. He had said, We do.

The fog grew thicker, and a mist began. They could barely see the searchers on either side of them. The fog muffled the sound of crashing brush, but muffled their voices, too. It was a tunnel of damp.

James was watching Lauren out of the corner of his eye. "Remember to look up," Flynn heard him say. "You have to keep checking the trees."

"I am looking up."

"You're not. And you're not moving things aside enough. You have to search *under* things."

"You can't look under everything. It's impossible."

"It's not impossible. You have to be patient, you have to pay attention. Something, anything, could be here."

"Look, here's a feather." She held it up to him. "Did they have birds on board?"

She had been brittle these last months, and perhaps James had grown weary of ignoring the sharp edges, of biting his tongue to keep peace. At first, after the procedure, as they called it, she had wandered the house, unable to remember why she walked into one room before she thought of a reason to leave that one and walk into another. He'd been relieved when the restlessness had turned into a fury of domestic pursuits. But those, too, most of them, had gone unfinished, forgotten mid-task. Now she stood there with this feather, ragged and dark, outstretched to him.

"Why are you here if you're not interested?" he asked. "Why are you here if you're not serious?"

She tried to throw the feather into a snarl of vines, but it hung back, mocking her effort. "I don't know," she said. "I don't know why I'm here. I brought you your stupid inhaler, okay? I'm tired of you running away every weekend, just because you don't want to be with me. I'm tired of cleaning and painting and tidying as if that could make us stand it better. I'm tired of trying to make everything better."

Perhaps James saw, then, the drive and ambition, the part of her that needed to know what came next, the part he'd admired and thought he'd loved, the part that could not put their lives into the hands of the Almighty. It was this lack of faith he must have caught, like a disease, from living with her. And he hated it.

They started to move again, to catch up to the others. James swept his machete across a shrubby weed that was not in his path. His ankle was caught by a wiry vine and he thrashed at that, too, making a shallow slice in his boot. Lauren had come closer to him, encroaching on his ten-foot swath. She was talking to him, something about his failure to see the limits of God. She kept her voice low, but maybe it sounded to him like yelling, and then it sounded like screaming and then she got in the way of one of his patterned, predictable rhythmic swings. She stopped screaming and just stood, a spot of blood appearing on the leg of her jeans. He had caught her at the knee, her knee which had a dimple just in the middle, a dimple that had made him catch his breath the first time he saw it below her cut-offs—a charming, uncanny, beckoning inroad of flesh.

"Look what you did," Lauren cried. "You could have torn off my kneecap." She moved toward the safety of a tree and rolled up her pants leg. It was a small cut, a skin-deep nick.

"I've got Band-Aids," James said. He fumbled in a pocket. The line halted to wait for them. Flynn had rushed back to where they stood. "Man, what happened? You two have a fight?"

"No," James said. "We're fine."

Lauren sat against the tree, holding the leg of her rolled-up jeans, watching where a trickle of blood traveled toward her boot. James started to put two band-aids on her leg, but she grabbed them out of his hand and stretched them across the cut.

Flynn looked at the machete, then at James. "You got to be careful with those things, you know?"

"She ran into a briar," James said. "One of those." He pointed to a tall one with inch-long thorns. When he reached for Lauren's hand, she glanced at Flynn. James would have seen that because of pride and the way things looked to others, she let him pull her back to standing.

As Flynn walked off she rolled down her pants leg. "You stay on your side," she said. "Just stay away from me."

It could be that this was the point where James gave up on his dream, his idea that his life could be sweet and joyous, that he could be a modern man with a modern attitude about life and love and the lengths to which we can go, must go, to prove that we care for one another. It could be, that if he'd come to the woods week after week and searched up as well as down, hour after tedious hour, and in the end found nothing of significance, that he might have been all right. He might have returned to the ordinary issues of home and marriage, the routine of whose turn it was to empty the trash or put away the dishes, and he would have been all right.

But James did not leave the woods empty-handed that day. In the weeds ahead of him—ahead of all of them—was a four-foot chunk of the shuttle's windshield, driven two feet into the soil by the force of its return to earth beside a swampy spot in Izzy Blanchard's far pasture. I can only surmise that this great find, this trophy of a ruin, did not bring James what he was looking for, or what he needed. I can only imagine that after the hoopla and the celebrating and the waiting around for NASA to come and claim its prize, that James discovered that he was still in the same unhappy place he had been when he started.

It was then that James did something quite beyond the pale, quite beyond what any of us who knew him might have expected: He stole the only survivors of this tragedy, which tore from their cabinet, fell twenty-six miles through the atmosphere and landed in a bit of Virginia creeper under a beech tree. As the sun, which had been hidden all day, came out in the late afternoon, a shaft of light found its way through the trees, a glow that caught the edge of a Petri dish, full of yellow liquid. James was a little ways from his fellow searchers, taking a pee behind some bushes. The bright thing caught his eye. When he finished his business, he picked up the Petri dish, the label *C. elegans* still on it, and he saw that it must be teeming with life. I believe that when he held the bit of miracle he perceived a moment of such significance that he slipped the dish into his pocket and folded his hands in prayer. He did not know that Flynn, too, had answered a call of nature and was a few yards behind him, close enough to see not what James took, but that he took. My friend Flynn is not a cruel man, but he had seen enough of James—not the real James, but the angry, grieving, off-balance James— that instead of confronting the thief with what he had seen—which I believe he might have done on a normal day, but this certainly was not one of those—Flynn went to the authorities. When James headed for the parking lot that night with the nematodes in his pocket, a sheriff's deputy was there to meet him.

James could not give them a reason then, nor could he give one to Lauren when she saw him later, while we waited for his bail to be set. It can take everything you have to please those you cherish and respect, especially if one of them is God. I am not a particularly religious man—in that way I am more like Mr. Armstrong than James—but I believe that we all must find the frame that gives our lives meaning. Otherwise, what is left for you, when someone you once knew dies suddenly in her garden, and you must go to your garage where you can be alone, where through many years you can be alone, because you cannot, will not, explain to your wife how it came to be that this distant death has torn a fragment from your soul, and sent it sailing into the hereafter.

# PASTURE, STUBBLE, SHOULDER OF THE HIGHWAY

She was a bit of a free spirit, his wife. Not your run-of-the-mill preacher's mate. Pastor Will Simpson knew his congregation, some of them, at least, thought Holly MacFarland and her long wild hair had brushed against the devil's ways. Her first husband had turned out to be gay. Also, there was her yoga studio, a shady bit of spiritual business. The members of Spring Creek Baptist might have chosen differently for the second wife of Pastor Simpson, but he loved her with all his heart.

Holly had closed her yoga studio—Kiser could not support it—but a little group of them still met on Saturdays, here at the house. Soon they would be coming up the walk in their flowing tops and unfettered pants. Simpson still had tomorrow's sermon to write, and the women would

KATHRYN SCHWILLE

talk, and they would now take over the den, which had the most floor space and also his favorite chair. He'd typed a few words from Job on his laptop screen: *His wealth will become hunger.* Thanksgiving was next week.

Simpson had married Holly on the rebound, his critics would say, two years after her divorce. She had come into the marriage with a large, stubborn pony and a smart but troubled boy. It seemed to Simpson that he'd spent his whole short marriage trying to connect with the child. He loved Frankie but was relieved when, after totaling Holly's car in a wreck a year ago—the day after Thanksgiving—Frankie had moved to Houston to live with his father. That left Simpson and Holly with most of this year to themselves. He'd expected it to be different.

The pony was still with them and Simpson could see him from the den window, staring at his pasture when he should have been eating from it. Drought had brought Texas to its knees; the fields were devoid of grass. There was no hay anywhere in the state, a drought like this not seen since the fifties. Rosco's new diet was all processed, too expensive by far, and still he was chewing on the fence posts.

Holly came into the room and spread out her yoga mat. Simpson helped her move the coffee table to a corner. "I'm sorry, honey," she said. "You mind going in the kitchen?"

He could smell her shampoo in the damp frizz around her shoulders, a grapefruit scent that wouldn't linger, though he would not have minded if it did. When they were first married, they would take long showers together and his fingers would be greedy for the slick, lathered

174

abundance of her hair. Soaping her bottom, or her breast, he would wonder how Wes MacFarland could not have wanted her, the way any normal man would. His early sex with her was ferocious, desperate and frequent. She was the most exciting woman he'd ever been with, and she had competition in that regard. Simpson was tall, and some said handsome, dark auburn hair when he was young, a slender build going only a little soft now. He had answered the call later than most.

Holly set a portly beige candle in the center of the room and lit it. Now he smelled sandalwood, which he disliked. "Seems like a nice day," he said. "I'll go hide out at the church." He didn't have an office there—the church was too small for that—but it was a warm fall day and there was a bench by the cemetery.

"If you hadn't left it to the last minute," she said. "You weren't even teaching this week."

"I know."

This was old territory. He procrastinated about the sermons. He was a part-time minister; pastoral inspirations came and went as they pleased. His other job, substitute teacher, came and went, too. The teachers had been remarkably healthy this year, with no emergency surgeries or problem pregnancies. He wouldn't wish the flu on anyone, but he could wish for the women—the married ones, of course—to be more fertile.

"I'm a sloth. And you're a good preacher's wife."

"So they tell me. What are you writing this week?"

"About hunger, I think."

"Mmm. Nice." She gave him the smile that said, I'm about to ask you for something. Her usual smile was girl-next-door-bright, like a model in an outdoor catalog. This other displayed the slightest tension at the corners. He often wondered if Wes MacFarland had found her so telegraphic.

"Could you stop by the feed store?" she asked.

"Again?"

"He has to eat. There's nothing in his—" she hesitated. "Nothing in his pasture." When he met her, she would occasionally curse. *Nothing in his damn pasture.* "He needs roughage. He needs his hay. Look how pointy his croup is. He didn't look like that six months ago. I mean he's older, yes, but his ribs shouldn't be showing like that."

"Poor guy. So more alfalfa pellets. How many bags?"

"How many can we afford? He's going through one a week."

Simpson had not yet told her that his church salary would be fifteen percent less next year. The Great Recession, as people were calling it now, plus the drought, had bit deeply. Collections were down and the deacons had been firm. He could hardly complain. Some in his congregation had lost their jobs. The salary cut, when he got around to telling her, would trigger a round of frugal, meatless meals. She felt guilty that her job at the furniture store, tied to commissions, paid so little.

Holly had read the look on his face. "We should give him away. We could find a good home for him." Her own face said, I'm saying this but I don't mean it.

"Who would take him? We don't know anybody rich enough, who doesn't already have animals of their own." Ranchers were selling off cattle they couldn't feed. The horse rescue place down in Yellowpine was swamped. Horses were being abandoned, dropped off like puppies, or worse, left in barren pastures to starve.

Simpson closed his laptop. It made more of a snap than he intended. "We should have found a home for him when Frankie outgrew him." All their disagreements came back to Frankie, even when he wasn't here.

"I know, sweetie. You're right. By the way, I got a text. He says he won't be here 'til Thanksgiving afternoon."

"But we're having dinner at two."

"We can have dinner after he gets here."

"It's not what we planned."

They were not having an argument, exactly. It did not feel like that. It felt like the edges of one were in view, and they were skating toward it. Out the window Simpson could see Jenny Lockwood coming up the walk in jeans that wrapped snugly around her thighs. She carried a pair of soft pants over her arm. The women used his and Holly's bedroom to change out of their street clothes. Really, he had no place to be when they came.

"I need to get this done," he said. He kissed Holly on the cheek, picked up his jacket and slipped out the back door.

"I bought steaks for dinner," she called.

Outside, Rosco stood head-down, tail to the gate, one hind hoof tilted in rest. Thirst had settled over the landscape for one more day. The variegated fields were all one color now—the pastures, the stubble and the dry clay shoulder of the highway were all the pale-bark hue of an ash tree. It was as if the seeds of normal bounty had been blown away. The pony lifted his head expectantly as Simpson crossed the drive to his truck, and the minister opened his hand. "Nothing for you," he said. A neighbor girl had been riding him; she would bring a carrot or a mint. What else did the old boy have to look forward to?

Holly had maintained, right from the start, that she had little interest in the traditional roles of a minister's wife, and Simpson had thought he would be okay with that. The women of the congregation didn't warm to her, and she was dismissive of the ones who fawned over their preacher, as church women sometimes do. Lately, she had begged off attending services at the slightest excuse, and he would find her at home, in some pose or another. Simpson had tried hard not to tell her, not too often at least, that if she would just give her troubles to God, He could help. Was it true he had married her thinking he could save her? He'd counseled others, many times, not to fall into that trap. Last night, he'd awakened to the sound of her quiet weeping. She'd burrowed her face into the pillow just behind his head. He could discern the rise and fall of her breasts as she took her ragged, irregular breaths. He knew he should have asked what the trouble was and reached out for her. It was part of his job, after all, to attend to others' tears. Instead, he feigned sleep and left her there in the dark alone. Outside, he'd heard thunder.

A storm had been forecast for today; Simpson was sure it would not come. He guessed that Holly's trouble was Frankie, and he didn't want to hear it again. Frankie had not been back to Kiser in two months, and now he was going to breeze in late to Thanksgiving. Simpson did not want to criticize Holly's parenting, but if Frankie had been better grounded in religion, he might not have ended up with so many issues. Frankie had an interior life, overly developed in Simpson's opinion, and it did not include prayer. Simpson had tried to talk to him about prayer, but he could tell the boy was only humoring him. Frankie would politely go through the motions. Yes, I should do that. Yes sir.

"Does he even like me?" Simpson had asked Holly, after they'd been married a few months.

"We'll never know what he's thinking," she said. "Not exactly. You know, for a kid, he's kind of a deep thinker. He likes you, I'm sure. I see that, don't you?"

Simpson had not. He wondered what would be different, now that Frankie had received nearly a year of expensive counseling—secular counseling—paid for by Ben, the man Wes lived with, a man Simpson could not call boyfriend, partner, lover or any of those terms that implied intimacy. He thought it a dangerous setting to raise a boy and wondered if Frankie might be gay, like his father. If that were true, Simpson felt sorry for him. He did not think gay people should be persecuted, but he did not court their company.

"What if he turns?" he'd asked Holly, before Frankie moved.

"Turns?"

"You know, living with two gay men."

"Oh, Will. Please don't. You preach love. You preach it all the time. It's how I love you best." Still, she once had made him swear that he had never been, and never would be, attracted to a man. He had assured her he had no doubts.

"Why was it you got divorced?" she'd asked, when they were first dating.

He could not tell her the truth. His wife had left him for another. She was married now to a man, but she had pursued this other thing, briefly, with a woman, and it had humiliated him. Now, it gave him a bond with Holly that only he knew the depth of, a bizarre, incredulous link he turned over in his mind many times.

"We didn't love each other anymore," he'd answered.

"It's okay then, I guess, when you don't have kids."

"I think, in God's eyes, it's not okay."

She had reached for his hand then, and covered it with her own. "Forgive yourself," she said. It was at that moment he knew, he could love this woman.

He tried not to be troubled when, on occasion, Holly accidentally called him Wes. Not in times of intimacy, but in the off-hand, could-you-take-out-the-garbage kind of way, the thoughtless moment of that other name starting with a W. She would laugh. He would wince. It had occurred to him that he might be insecure, vaguely threatened by a man who wasn't around. They were on good terms, she and Wes. They had Frankie to think about.

There was always Frankie to think about. Holly was attuned to his moods—of which there were many—and set out to ease the stepfather notion as much as she could. Wes had sent money, early on, for them to buy Frankie a used piano. Holly thought it would be a good outlet for him, when she and Simpson were first married. Frankie had shown some talent, if not enthusiasm. The sight-reading came easily to him—one more thing, like school, that did not challenge him. Simpson had overheard him talking to a friend after practicing. His teacher assigned simple tunes. This week's was insipid: "For He's a Jolly Good Fellow."

Frankie told his friend he was bored with piano.

"Then why do you do it?" Josh was the kind of kid who liked to stir things up.

"I don't know. Mom wants me to."

"Man, you're such a pushover."

"She's had a hard time."

Simpson had felt it then, a pang of jealousy, a sour note in the counter-melody. Frankie was devoted to Holly, and she to him. That night he had made love to her fiercely, that silly song an ear worm in his brain. The b-flat that Frankie sometimes missed was in there, too.

❋ ❋ ❋

When Simpson had made the rounds of the church—
checked the doors, picked up the mail—he discovered yet another dime bag hidden in a backside downspout. He'd found the little bags before, and was no closer to knowing what to do this time than last. The others he had tossed, scattering their seedy contents into the woods or under a pile of moldering leaves. Today though, he was inclined to watch and wait. From the bench beside the cemetery, he would have a good view of the dirt-and-gravel road leading to the church. He knew he couldn't stop the trade, not without seeing someone go to jail, and he didn't want that. Did that make him a liberal? Not wanting to see someone go to jail for trafficking? You could not build a fence against the devil. Dime bags were everywhere; it was the spirit that needed fortification.

Arthur Kenny's pickup was parked behind the cemetery, a tarp covering something in the bed. Arthur was in the graveyard, as he was most Saturdays, tending his son's grave, tidying up others. His brindle hound, churning around outside the cemetery, bounded up to Simpson. The dog had long canines for her size. Simpson put out his hand for a sniff.

Arthur called out. "You ain't afraid are you? She don't bite."

"Won't bother me."

Simpson settled on the bench under the big oak and opened the laptop. The cemetery, bone-dry, looked not much different from usual. It was a swept cemetery, every blade of grass plucked out. Last night's wind had blown the dust into shallow waves; Arthur Kenny's boots had left footprints. Beneath Simpson's feet, wild hogs had rooted for acorns, their hooves leaving prints in the clay where even the wire grass had given up trying to grow. His toe nudged a clump of dislodged moss that had dried in shape, like a starfish washed beyond the tide's reach. The landscape was faded country now, its spirit wearied by thirst and betrayal. Above the horizon, gray clouds, light and crazy in shape, formed like dust bunnies. Every afternoon for a week the clouds had gathered but not spilled. Minden Lake was so low that grass grew where grownups used to wade knee-deep. A four-foot cryogenic tank had appeared, debris from the shuttle that had come apart eight years ago. The drought was a quieter disaster, with no litter from the sky or failing banks.

"They're omnivores, you know," Arthur said, coming toward the bench where Simpson had just finished typing the line from Job. *His wealth will become hunger, and disaster is ready for his stumbling.* Arthur threw a stick for the dog to chase. "They're digging for grubs."

Simpson noticed a new slump to Arthur Kenny's shoulders. He and his wife hadn't graced a pew at Spring Creek Baptist in months. Simpson had lost a few parishioners to Trinity Baptist, where Rev. Roland Purser preached a gospel of prosperity. He suspected Arthur was one of these lost lambs. He decided to pick at the wound.

"We haven't seen you much lately, Arthur." The dog had bounded back and now dropped the stick at Arthur's feet, taking the edge of his jeans between her showy teeth. "You thinking of leaving us?"

Arthur nudged the dog off his leg and threw the stick

again, harder this time, toward the back of the church. She covered the ground with fiendish speed. "If we picked up all the acorns, wouldn't be no reason for them to be here at all, the hogs. Not many acorns this year, anyhow."

"I'm just going to say it outright, if you'll forgive me," Simpson said. "There's other churches, I know. There's other ministers that offer something different. But we can't pray our way to better fortune. We can pray for rain, and we do, and maybe God is interested in whether our crops grow and we have hay for our creatures. But this praying for worldly goods, for money to buy things, it just doesn't work."

"Heard on the radio that Texas lost a million trees so far. See where the bark's sloughing off this oak. Canker fungus. Comes from stress."

Simpson marveled at the metaphorical significance of this non-conversation. Purser was rooting around in Simpson's flock and gobbling up the weak ones. Simpson thought he had prepared them better for the assaults of the world, nourishing them with thoughtful sermons. Each defection felt like a failure. He knew Purser's preaching was more—what was the phrase? Full-throttle.

"Dammit Dingo. Get out of there." The dog, exploring the back of the church, had stuck her nose in the gutter where the dime bag nestled. Arthur stood up so quickly he nearly tumbled. "Come here, girl." Simpson started to say something, but what could he say? Admit he knew what was hidden there?

"Excuse my language, preacher. Dog pokes her nose

into everything. Dingo, get over here." The dog pulled out of the downspout. "She's looking for a chipmunk. Plays with them like a cat with a mouse. She got anything in her mouth?"

"Doesn't look like it."

Arthur walked over to inspect the dog. He pushed his fingers into her mouth, between her back teeth. She let out a cry. "You hear about what they found at the lake, now it's so low?"

Again, they were off topic. There seemed to be no way to turn the tide. "A cryogenic tank," Simpson said. "From the shuttle. I heard." There'd been a dime bag in the gutter that day, too, the day the shuttle fell. It had been an awful day, the church grounds littered with a mess they weren't allowed to clear, a newly-pregnant bride in tears, her day of joy ruined, her stupefied guests attempting cheer. An astronaut's heart would be found in the woods, and the dime bag rooted out later, too, as NASA set up a make-shift morgue at the church.

"No, the other thing. A car in the lake. A body inside it." Arthur settled onto the bench again and was about to shake a Camel out of its pack. Simpson hadn't remembered that he smoked. Maybe he was returning to an old habit, like Holly, who had started smoking again—in secret, though he could smell it on her. It was one more thing he needed to bring up with her and didn't want to.

"It's a skeleton by now I reckon," Arthur said. "You mind?" He held up the cigarette. Simpson shook his head, though he did, in fact, mind. "Turns out," Arthur said, "it's that Vickers woman disappeared three, four years ago. The one everyone thought just drove off somewheres and got herself a new life."

Suzanne Vickers. Her daughter Ally, from her marriage to that nasty Carl Hubble, had died in a swimming accident.

"Looks like she killed herself. Just drove into the lake. Right about where the girl drowned."

"My God," Simpson said. Suzanne's parents had been the first to flee his congregation for the prosperity gospel. This new grief of theirs was in Purser's hands now. Like their loyalty, they had transferred their need. Her disappearance had broken them. Simpson had encouraged them to believe she was okay, that she might even come home. Perhaps they had known, in their hearts, how wrong he was.

"Blessed are those who mourn," Simpson said. He would visit them, offer the comfort he had failed them before. He would need to bring the sad news into his sermon. "Her family, they need our prayers. They really do. Will you do that, Arthur? Will you pray for them?" He wanted to add, will you put aside your other praying, those petitions to fill your life? He thought he'd better change the subject, before he began to, as Holly would say, preach where it wasn't wanted.

The dog had rushed off again and now was back at the bench, licking Simpson's hand. Everyone wanted forgiveness. "What's that you've got under the tarp in your truck?"

"Got a few bales of hay."

"Where in the world did you get them?"

"This old boy I know has a connection in Kentucky. He's been keeping it locked up in his barn. You need some? You still keeping that pinto? I can spare you four, five bales."

Simpson figured the price would be out of reach. But Holly would be pleased if he scored some hay. He wanted to cheer her. It would be like the first Christmas they were dating and he'd found the video game Frankie wanted most in a lucky moment on Amazon, just before they sold out.

"Let me see it." They walked over to Arthur's pickup, where a blue tarp was fastened with a bungee cord over the precious haul. Hay was so scarce in Texas that a group of farmers in Indiana had sent truckloads to Eno last month to give away, like a bread line. Arthur unfastened a corner of the tarp and threw it back.

"What kind is it?" Simpson was bluffing here. He didn't know one kind of hay from another, but he knew this hay didn't smell like freshly mown grass. The hay was stemmy, and probably old, he knew that much.

"Alfalfa."

"Looks like last year's," Simpson said.

"Might be. He'll eat it though. They're not picky when they're hungry. I give it to you for ten bucks a bale. About what I paid for it."

Simpson was sure that wasn't true, but he let it go. Roughage, Holly kept saying. He has to have roughage. They transferred the bales to Simpson's pickup.

"I'm obliged, Arthur," Simpson said, and put out his hand. "'Til next time? Out here, I guess, by the graves? Not in a pew?"

"The wife," Arthur said. "She wanted the change."

When Simpson arrived home, Jenny's car was in the driveway, which meant yoga might still be in session, so he unloaded the hay into the little barn they'd built for Rosco. It felt like a fruitful day. After Arthur had driven off, Simpson wrote a note and put it in the downspout: *God loves you and forgives you.* Simpson trusted his instincts about the way Arthur had reacted to the dog's snooping. He'd folded the note and written on the front: To A.K.

Now he peeled off a big flake of hay and spread it into the pasture, which brought Rosco running. After Jenny drove off, Holly came out to the field.

"You found hay at the feed store? I don't believe it."

"Arthur Kenny was at the church. Had some in his truck."

They watched Rosco's gleeful eating. "Is it all this stemmy?" she said.

"Kind of."

"I suppose beggars can't be choosey. How much was it?"

"Not too much. Considering."

"Did you look it over good?" It wasn't great hay, and soon she would tell him that. She'd always taken good care of her animals. He followed her into the barn.

"Arthur told me they've found something else at the lake," he said. "Besides that tank from the shuttle. They found Suzanne Vickers's car."

"I thought they'd searched all around there." She was re-arranging the bales, turning them over, looking closely. "This might be older than last year even. I thought they'd dragged the lake."

"The thing is, they found Suzanne's body inside. She must have driven it in there."

"What?"

"At the spot where her little girl drowned."

Holly held up some of the hay she'd pulled out of a bale. He wasn't sure she had heard him.

"Damn. I don't believe it. You didn't."

"Didn't what?"

She plucked something from the hay. It was a slender, brown stalk, a fuzzy bloom on it. "My God, Will," she cried. "He can't eat this. It's full of foxtail. It's worse than nothing."

Holly threw down the stem and hurried out to the pasture where Rosco was eating. She pitched his little pile of hay over the fence where he couldn't reach it. The poor animal grabbed what he could as she took it.

Will followed her to the fence. "You're throwing it out?"

"He slicked you into buying this. Foxtail's a weed. It has burrs that gives them sores in their mouths. Didn't you look at it? Arthur Kenny knows better. He had to know. What a slimebag jerk."

"I'm sure he didn't know."

"How much, Will? How much did you pay for this crap?"

"Arthur will take it back. I know he will. I'll get six bags of alfalfa pellets. Six bags will hold us for a while."

She covered her face with her hands. Was she going to cry again? Over hay? "What am I going to do?"

"I'll go to the feed store. I'll go right now."

Her shoulders were shaking. "You just don't get it, do you?"

"Get what? I made a mistake, I'm sorry. I can fix it."

"No. You can't fix it. Nobody can fix it. Don't you see? She lost her child. She *lost* her child."

Slowly, he made the connection. He shouldn't have told her, not so off-handedly. "But we still have Frankie. He got hurt, but he didn't die. He's okay, Frankie is. And you're not Suzanne. She had a hard life. Two husbands that abused her. A lot of problems. And Frankie is still with us."

Another mistake. She was bent over now, and would not look at him. Rosco was nosing the ground, desperate for another nibble. Simpson fumbled on. "I mean he's still on this earth. Not that far away. We still have him." It had been a close call with Frankie. Holly believed he aimed the car at a tree; Simpson was not so sure. Frankie said he was drunk and blacked out, though the tests did not confirm this. He had been lucky, in terms of injuries; the car hit on the passenger's side. He'd had a concussion, three broken ribs, a broken leg.

"That's just it," Holly said. "We don't have him. Frankie would have lived with me." Now she was looking at him. "He didn't want to live with us."

Simpson gathered his breath. "That's what you think? Think of what all he's got now. A car, nice clothes, a cell phone and a brand new computer. His father has better toys. Trappings he doesn't need, by the way. What kid wouldn't want that?"

"You were always pushing religion on him."

"Well he didn't get much growing up, did he?"

Simpson knew he'd gone too far. She turned away and walked toward the house, crawling through the barbed wire fence to avoid the gate where he stood. "I know you did the best you could," he called after her. "Holly, please."

He watched her go, knowing it was better to stay than to follow. He picked up a stalk of the brown weed and ran his finger down its foxy bloom. It was soft on the outside, but inside, by the stalk, it was burry, like a thistle. He put the bloom in his mouth and ran it across the inside of his lip, pressed it to the inside of his cheek. A little piece came out and gripped itself there. He left the hay where it was and headed to the feed store. He would deal with Arthur Kenny later.

Shortly before Frankie's accident, Simpson had left the house one night to lead the bible study. Holly was at her father's, fixing dinners to put in his freezer. It had been two years since Cloyd's wife had died, and still she was feeding him. Simpson was almost to the church when he realized he'd left his notes at home, so he double backed. Pulling into the drive he saw a light move in the barn. Then it went out. Simpson pulled a flashlight from the glove box. Before he even got to the barn he smelled the dope. He shined the light right into Frankie's face. The mop of dark hair—so like Wes's mother, according to everyone—fell defiantly over one eye. The boy did not even look sheepish.

"How long has this been going on?" Simpson asked.

"It was just this one, I swear."

"I don't believe you. What else have you been doing out here?"

"Nothing. Nothing else."

"Where'd you get it?"

"Some guy at school. Just this one, I swear."

"Stop swearing."

Simpson flicked the light on in the barn. "As God is my witness, Frankie, I have tried with you. I have tried to understand you, I have tried to present a good example for you. I have tried to love you, and I do love you, but I will not have you become an embarrassment to your mother, to me or to the church."

"Are you going to tell Mom?"

"Of course I'm going to tell her."

"It was just this one. Don't tell her. Please don't tell her."

"So now you're thinking about your mother? You mean more to her than anything else in the world. Anything. You get that?" Holly was always worried about him. What would he do, what was he thinking, how could they reach him, how could they get him to open up, what did he do when he walked in the woods alone. Simpson was tired of it. As long as Frankie was in the house, Holly would be preoccupied, vulnerable to his moods, his brooding behind the closed bedroom door—what was he doing, what was he thinking.

"You know what?" Simpson said. "I've had it. I'll do you a favor. I won't tell her. It would break her heart. But here's what I want from you. I want you out of here. I want you to tell her that you want to live with your father. Go down there and live in that house of ridiculous morals. Be whoever it is you want to be or whoever it is you think you are, because you weren't made to live around here."

Frankie stormed past him toward the door, yelling over his shoulder. It was the most emotion Simpson had heard from the boy in a year. "We were fine. Until you came along, her and me. We were fine."

Simpson had half expected Frankie to confess to Holly. But he had not. The day after Thanksgiving he announced that he had enough credits to graduate from high school in December, and then he would leave. Simpson had not been home when he said it, and came home to find Holly in tears. That night Frankie asked to borrow Holly's car to visit his friend Josh. Wherever he went, he didn't go to Josh's. They got the call about ten. A week after Frankie was released from the hospital, he left for Houston. He didn't come home for his graduation, or for Christmas.

Simpson knew he had spoken in a sinful anger, but he believed at the time, and still did, that God had guided him to what was best, painful as it was, even though he'd sent the boy into a lion's den of sin. Holly had told him once: I love him so much, I have to hide it, how much I do. Now Simpson had bribed her boy away, like a father clearing out his daughter's unsuitable beau. He had tried to console Holly about the move. "He needs counseling, and Ben can pay for that," he said. "We don't have people around here for what he needs. It could end up to be a good thing."

This had not consoled her. If she was preoccupied with Frankie's moods before, she became more unhappy without him. Instead of coming more often to church, she came less. Instead of more sex, they had less. Simpson knew he had been selfish, and he was paying for it.


They already had said the Thanksgiving blessing when Frankie pulled up. Out the window they could see he was driving the used pickup his father—or more likely Ben—had bought him. Simpson was worried about Frankie's visit, and had not wanted to share the precarious dinner with a crowd, but Holly's irascible father was there.

"Sorry I'm late," Frankie said. His mother filled a plate for him and he dug right in.

Simpson put up his hand. "We've said grace, Frankie. We'll wait while you say one for yourself." Frankie bowed his head, and Simpson saw his lips move. What were they saying? Could be the lyrics to a popular song. The boy had a new gold stud in his left ear. Holly's father could not resist. While Frankie wasn't looking, Cloyd made a face, pointing to his own ear. Holly shot him a warning look. Simpson tried to remember, was the left ear the one that said, I'm gay?

"The turkey's a little dry," Holly said. "I'm sorry."

"It's perfect, Mom," Frankie said. The small compliment brought the girl-next-door smile to her face. She had brightened the moment Frankie arrived. Now he pulled an iPhone from his pocket. Holly had planned to give him one for Christmas.

"That's new," Holly said. "Your dad give you that?"

"Ben."

"I think you should put that up while we're eating," Simpson said. Why was he always the heavy? Holly should have said it.

Frankie turned the phone over but kept it on the table. His insolent, teenage energy hung in the air, exactly as Simpson remembered.

The weather was a safe topic. They clung to that for a while. Cloyd prattled on about crop losses, the hay, the months since rainfall and the drought of the fifties, which he recalled in detail.

"That tree at Parker's where Frankie found the astronaut," Cloyd said. "Got a bunch of dead limbs on it. That whole patch there, won't survive if we don't get rain."

"We're supposed to get a shower today," Simpson said. He'd heard a forecast, probably wrong again.

"Rosco's thin," Frankie said.

"Every horse in Texas is thin," Cloyd said. He was studying Frankie's stud again. "Your father got an earring?"

"No. No, he doesn't. But Ben's got two."

"You got a girlfriend?" Cloyd asked.

"Dad." Holly put down her fork and picked up the potatoes. "Anyone want more?"

"Just asking. Any harm in taking an interest? Pass me that dressing."

"Maybe I got a boyfriend," Frankie said. He tapped his stud. "You know."

"He's not serious," Simpson said.

"I don't see how that's something to joke about," Cloyd said. "It's not funny."

"Not meant to be," Frankie said.

Simpson was sure if the boy were gay, this would not be his way of telling them. "Show your grandfather more respect."

Frankie looked at him. "You going to tell me to leave again?"

Simpson could not utter a word. Out of the corner of his eye he could see that Holly was watching him. For a long minute, no one said anything.

Frankie asked to be excused. Holly was still staring at Simpson. "Dad," she said. "Why don't you go make yourself comfortable in the den. The remote's by the recliner. I'm sure there's football. We'll have dessert later." She began picking up plates. "Need help?" Simpson asked.

She didn't answer. He waited a moment, trying to decide how to proceed. He picked up two glasses and followed her into the kitchen. "What should I do?" It was a poor choice of words.

She was filling the dishwasher.

"Are you okay?"

"Fine."

"I love him, you know," he said. "But I love you more. Is that so awful?"

She was staring at him again. Had she guessed? If not the deal, then the asking. Here was the end to months of wondering if Frankie would mention it, surprise and relief that he had not. Simpson had prepared for the moment when he might have to say the boy didn't have his story straight, that he had made something up. That he had misunderstood.

"Sweetheart. He had an accident. It was just that, an accident. It could have happened any time, any night of our lives."

"Could you please collect the napkins and put them in the laundry room."

As soon as he left the kitchen he heard a dish fall to the floor. He poked his head back in.

"It's the dressing," she said. "I'll get it. Just pick up the napkins." She bent over the dish on the floor, scooping dressing into a paper towel. "Just the napkins."

Simpson walked around the dining room table, picking up, and heard the back door close. In the kitchen, he saw paper towels and dressing scattered across the floor. The flowered dish was broken in two. It had been his mother's, a hand-painted favorite they brought out for holidays and company. He put the pieces in the trash and wiped the floor where the dressing had left greasy spots. He stood, then, at the back door, looking out. It had begun to rain. He could see the two of them in the barn, fussing over the pony. Holly was combing Rosco's mane; Frankie was on the other side, brushing his neck. They were a family, the three of them. Simpson was the outsider and always would be. He could see that.

The downpour arrived, water washing uselessly over the hard landscape. If the wind rose, the weakened limbs and roots of the trees would give way, a storm worse than nothing. He watched them in their ministrations, hoping one of them would turn his way.

# SLIVER OF MOON

Not a cloud. Plato Winchester spreads out on a quilt in the grass, studies the stars over his piece of Texas. Carina, Dorado, Hydra, Tucana. Orion's belt. That nebula, M42. The camper behind him, shelter to all he owns, holds the tiny book of stars, companion since grade school, memorized and finger-worn. A gift from fat Aunt Grace. He has named a star for her, the spinster aunt who showered him with love. There in the point of Draco's tail, Grace's Light. Sliver of moon, not a cloud. No devil can chase his happiness this January night; it is big as a bear, his joy. Ursa Major, Ursa Minor, Crater, Corvus, Centaurus. The yellow cur beside him presses a leg to his thigh—Pip, the youngest, snoring. His fingers find a scab on her leg. She is silent on the trail, his best pup yet. A coyote calls, the canebrake rustles. Tree toads there will sing another hour. He does not count the minutes, he with the clock in his head he needed once, and does not need now. He is a fortunate man. The loam is damp beneath him. Up there is what he loves. The tonight show, the night show, the late show, his only show. He thanks his lucky stars and there they are. Cathedral of stars, wishes on a star. All the cliches, here they are. He worships at the Church of Milky Way, glitter off God's crown. Andromeda Aries Auriga Orion. Winter's ripe for meteors. Something slips across the sky, northwest, just below Canopus. A lighted object, moving fast. He watches the tail of it glide away.

# AT THE WINDOW

Sliver of moon, the clouds are parting. Michael Kirkland wraps his legs around the pilot's seat of the craft that carries him, weightless through the heavens. He has floated forward, close as he can to his window in the sky. Alone at the end of his work day, and what he sees, oh what he sees, he drinks like a drug. Ten minutes to cross America. California lights, Mohave dark, neon Las Vegas. There are the Rockies, there are the plains. Pinch me, oh Lord. Is tonight more splendid than last? Phoenix, Albuquerque, Amarillo Shawnee. I-40, a serpent's lighted tail. There is Tulsa, where high school was. There is Owasso, the place of his birth. So far below, on gravity's sphere, all that he has ever loved. A mother, a girlfriend, old friends and a house. The crew in Houston, that clan of big dreamers. What luck this life of his. Oh speck of earth, how fast you pass. Oklahoma Missouri Kentucky New York. Zip the lights of Boston, zip the coast of Maine, they're gone. A check of the watch, life a clock up here. One more minute at the window. Sweet night. Here comes London, here comes Spain. Lord, I am a fortunate man. Sea to shining sea, I am.

*** *** ***

# ACKNOWLEDGMENTS

I 'm grateful to many people in East Texas who told me their stories so that I could tell mine. I was especially lucky to meet Jerry Nickerson, whose help and hospitality stretched beyond measure. Thanks also to Liz Ware, Kay Kutch, Charles Sharp and the Go-Texans. Marsha Cooper and Belinda Gay took me to the nose cap landing site. Sue Friday offered guidance in Charlotte and respite at her dog-trot house.

For technical aspects of the disaster, I was guided by the report from the Columbia Accident Investigation Board and *Comm Check: The Final Flight of Shuttle Columbia,* by Michael Cabbage and William Harwood. An account of the heroic efforts to recover crew remains and debris appears in the 2018 book, *Bringing Columbia Home,* by retired shuttle launch director Michael D. Leinbach and Jonathan D. Ward.

It was a stroke of great fortune to have this book land with the talented, hard-working crew at Hub City Press: Meg Reid, Kate McMullen and founder Betsy Teter. It's been a pleasure.

I'm grateful to the editors of the following journals where sections of the book appeared: "FM 104" in *Memorious*; "Against the Sky" as "Wind and Rain" in *New Letters*, "Pasture, Stubble, Shoulder of the Highway" in *New Letters*; "Bostic's" as "White Birch" in *The Chicago Tribune's Printer's Row*; "A Camp in the Woods" as "Veil" in *storySouth*.

Work on this manuscript was supported by a generous grant from the North Carolina Arts Council and fellowships from the Virginia Center for Creative Arts and Hambidge Center for the Arts and Sciences. Thanks also to friends who provided shelter from distractions: Larry and Brenda Sorkin, and Susan Patterson and George Tyree.

It's hard to imagine a tribe more sustaining than the faculty, students and alumni of the MFA Program for Writers at Warren Wilson College. My thanks forever to Ellen Bryant Voigt for inventing such a marvel. I'm grateful to faculty members Andrea Barrett, David Haynes, Kevin "Mc" McIlvoy and Peter Turchi for wisdom and patient support over the years. Special thanks to Mc for vision and push on this project. It would have been a lesser book without him.

I'm indebted to colleagues who read parts of this manuscript at crucial times: Donna Gershten, Marjorie Hudson, Alison Moore, Peg Alford Pursell, Geoff Kronik and Martha Brenner. Thanks also to Martha and the rest of the Writer Women—Jean Siers, Cheryl Spainhour, Fannie Flono and Suzanne Jeffries—for nights of riotous laughter and soulful friendship.

Words cannot express my appreciation for all the guides and healers who propelled me this far, especially Lynda Boozer and Brenda Sorkin. How profoundly different my life became through your work.

This book is in memory of my brother, Stephen—dreamer, pilot, aeronautical engineer. As kids we watched the launches, and seeds were sown.

Finally, none of this would have been possible without the encouragement, support and love of my extraordinary husband, Tom Lucas.

**HUB CITY**
PRESS

**HUB CITY PRESS** is a non-profit independent press in Spartanburg, SC, that publishes well-crafted, high-quality works by new and established authors, with an emphasis on the Southern experience. We are committed to high-caliber novels, short stories, poetry, plays, memoir, and works emphasizing regional culture and history. We are particularly interested in books with a strong sense of place.

Hub City Press is an imprint of the non-profit Hub City Writers Project, founded in 1995 to foster a sense of community through the literary arts. Our metaphor of organization purposely looks backward to the nineteenth century when Spartanburg was known as the "hub city," a place where railroads converged and departed.

## RECENT HUB CITY PRESS TITLES

*The Wooden King* • Thomas McConnell

*Whiskey & Ribbons* • Leesa Cross-Smith

*Ember* • Brock Adams

*Strangers to Temptation* • Scott Gould

*Over the Plain Houses* • Julia Franks

*Minnow* • James E. McTeer II

*Pasture Art* • Marlin Barton